Curse of the Zodiac

THE ZODIAC WARS
BOOK ONE

CURSE OF THE ZODIAC

THE ZODIAC WARS
BOOK ONE

Wayward Books
PUBLISHING

Curse of the Zodiac
Copyright © Yana Doering, 2022
All rights reserved.

First Canadian Edition

This is a work of fiction. Names, characters, places and incidents either are the product of the authors' imagination or are used fictitiously. Any resemblance to actual persons, living or dead, events, or locales is entirely coincidental.

All rights reserved. No part of this book may be reproduced in any form on by an electronic or mechanical means, including information storage and retrieval systems, without permission in writing from the publisher, except by a reviewer who may quote brief passages in a review.

www.yanakaplan39.wixsite.com/ashley-kaplan

Cover design by K.D. Ritchie
Interior artwork by: Zina Reinwald
Developmental edit by: Jonathan Oliver
Some line editing done by: Hana Blue

Title: Curse of the Zodiac / Ashley Kaplan
ISBN: 978-1-7777215-2-7 (softcover)
ISBN: 978-1-7777215-2-7 (ebook)

Printed by Amazon

Created by Wayward Books

Wayward Books
PUBLISHING

*To my sister Michelle,
My very own Zodiacs gift.*

✦ ◆ ✦

Pisces
Aries
Taurus
Gemini
Cancer
Leo
Virgo
Libra
Scorpio
Sagittarius
Capricorn
Aquarius

Beginning

Our world used to be ruled by the Zodiacs, god-like beings who watched and cared for our people. The gods provided clean water, green crops, and plenty of game in their benevolence. Every so often, if a Zodiac grew particularly fond of a mortal, those they considered true heroes, they would bestow a gift of their power onto them. These heroes became known as the Gifted.

Life was peaceful and humanity thrived until the Infernals attacked. It is said that the creatures were summoned from the darkest corners of the earth by the one we call the Cursed One, who was so enraged at being ignored by the Zodiacs that they sought power in the darkest of places.

No one is sure how the Cursed One gained their powers, only that the Infernals had been unleashed upon the world through them – creatures that were part man and part beast, with teeth like fangs and claws that were likened to daggers. They were savage beings; to be near them was to feel the cold grip of death. The Gifted were the only ones able to defend our people and fight back against the Infernals. And those who were willing to fight formed the Astral Army. The war between the two caused so much destruction on earth that, seeing this, the Zodiacs grew despondent. Some were incensed at the mortals for their nerve while others were sympathetic to their plight. But in the end, they all gave up on us one by one. Eventually, all of the Zodiacs retreated from the earth and fell into a deep slumber. Over time our abilities fell dormant in the absence of the gods. The Infernals crept into the shadows now that their enemies slept. Rivers ran dry as fields became wastelands of sand and dirt. The earth became unrecognizable and, with time, we forgot about things like gods and heroes. As we forgot about the real monsters that lurked in the shadows.

But some still believe our powers are just below the surface, waiting to awaken. They hope that the twelve Zodiacs will rise again one day, restoring our powers and returning the world to its former glory.

Ashley Kaplan

"Read it again!"

"Murphy, come on kid," I said, rolling my eyes. "No more procrastinating. It's bedtime."

I watched the ten-year-old hop out of his bed for the fifth time that night and run over to his bedroom window, looking up at the stars.

"Do you think they'll come back someday?" he asked in wonder.

I made a face at him and shook my head, coming up to stand behind him. He had a mop of dark brown hair, wide green eyes, a button nose, and a goofy grin as he daydreamed. Now if only I could get him in bed so that he would be dreaming for real.

"Murph, it's just a story, Zodiacs don't exist," I told him.

"My dad says they do."

I rolled my eyes again because of course Professor Abner would say that. He taught a course on ancient history at the local university. I wasn't sure if he actually believed that nonsense or if he was just humoring his son. For as long as I could remember it had just been the two of them. I don't know what happened to Mrs. Abner, the professor never talked about her and I wasn't about to ask Murphy. I had met the two of them when I was thirteen and started babysitting Murphy ever since. That was five years ago now. It felt like much longer. I was just a little girl back then, not that eighteen made me such an adult but I felt more like a woman now.

"That's just an old fairy tale Murph," I said.

"You don't believe in fairy tales?" a deep and familiar voice said behind me.

"Dad!" Murphy ran with open arms to hug his father in the doorway. Professor Abner was a fairly young father. He had laugh lines around his eyes and a straight-edged nose. His tanned complexion, dark eyes, and sleek black hair were so different from Murphy's that I could only assume he looked like his mother. He was slender in physique, wore a sweater vest almost exclusively, and always had the sleeves of his dress shirt rolled up to his elbows as he did now.

"Hop in bed buddy while I walk Arianna out, I'll be back in a minute."

Murphy nodded and waved me off. "Bye Ari!" he shouted.

I couldn't help but smile at him. "See you later kid."

Professor Abner walked me to the front door, pulling cash out of his wallet. There was a breeze coming in through the window behind him that had been left slightly ajar. The cool felt good in this heat.

"Here you go, how about we get you a cab?" he asked, handing me the cash.

"That's ok, I can walk, it's not that far from here."

Ashley Kaplan

Professor Abner put his hand to his chin, seeming deep in thought like he did during his lectures. I knew this look well since I attended his class.

"So why are you so sure that story is just a fairy tale?" he asked.

I was a little surprised at the question. "You can't be serious? Well, come on, like I would believe that some all-powerful beings who gave people powers existed! As if I could make magic happen with just a flick of my hand," I demonstrated and the window promptly slammed shut.

I looked stunned. Professor Abner just smiled kindly. "Just the wind."

I shook off the goosebumps that ran up my arms. "Right." I shook my head.

"Well, listen, you get home safe. I'll see you in class tomorrow?"

"Of course," I said, shaking my head. "Goodnight then. I'll see you tomorrow."

As I walked home, I couldn't help but think back to the story of the Zodiacs. It was a light and magical way to explain the world we lived in, but no more than that. The water supply in most towns was precarious at best. The fields between cities were nothing but dirt roads. The cities themselves though weren't so bad. People had learned to live with the little they had. Fruit-bearing trees were grown in labs to keep people fed, wells were being sunk, and people had found a way to survive. We had schools and hospitals, but there were few resources left to take care of our buildings and streets. Garbage littered the sidewalks and some buildings were falling into disrepair. The people did the best they could but it wasn't enough. Technology was helping us survive but our scientists had been trying for years to restore vegetation to the wastelands with no luck. No matter what they tried it was like the ground was cursed. I shook my head, scolding myself for letting the fairy tale get the better of me.

Rounding a corner, I was almost home and could see the building up ahead. I had been living alone in a one-bedroom apartment for the last six months, ever since I'd turned eighteen and left my foster parents. Allan and Margie were great people but I was finally an adult and ready to be out on my own. As soon as I turned eighteen I was given access to the small inheritance left to me by my parents. I was not rich by any means but it was enough to get me started as an independent adult and get my apartment with some money left over.

I remembered bits and pieces of my parents even though they passed when I was only eight. Their photographs helped me connect with the near-strangers. I saw my full bottom lips and high cheekbones on my mom. I had her wavy, thick, brown hair and hazel eyes while I'd inherited my dad's thin nose, rounded at the tip. Both of my parents were Colombian and one of the few things I remembered were some of the stories my mother used to tell me about their homeland. With no other family to claim me after they died, off into the system I went.

Ashley Kaplan

But I was one of the lucky ones. I haven't bounced around as much as some kids. My foster homes were always generous, even paying for my martial arts and boxing classes. Professor Abner gave me my first real job back then and he was also the one who helped me find my apartment. But I grew up taking family where I could get it, so it wasn't very surprising that I eventually came to feel that way about them.

I was almost home – steps away – when the hairs on the back of my neck stood up. The breeze had died down. I could hear crickets and suddenly I became very aware of how empty the streets were. My hand dug nervously in my pocket for my keys. I felt I needed to get off the street immediately as I fumbled to unlock the door. A rush of cold spread through my body; it didn't feel right, not in this humidity. I finally got the lock undone and flew into the building, slamming the door behind me. Taking a deep breath, I allowed the warmth from the hallway to seep into me. I didn't know what that had been all about; maybe I had let Murphy's stories get into my head, but I felt relieved to be home. I couldn't wait to get up to my apartment, crawl into bed, and fall asleep.

The next morning I met up with my friends, Joel and Katie, at the university, just as we did every weekday. Years back I had been placed with Katie's family for a while. Her parents were hippies and the best people I've ever met. There was no shortage of kindness and love in their home. It didn't take long for Katie and me to become inseparable. Joel was her best friend and often a dinner guest at their home. From those days on the three of us were a team.

"Hey guys," I said casually with a yawn.

Joel grinned and handed me a warm cup of heavenly coffee.

"Cutting it a little close aren't you?" he asked.

Closing my eyes, I inhaled the aroma of coffee and took a satisfying sip. "Just what I needed. I feel like I barely slept last night."

"Bad dream?" Katie asked with a sympathetic smile.

"I guess. I can't remember. Nothing that a little caffeine can't fix though."

We fell into step together, making our way to Professor Abner's class. The university was one of the only buildings that the city still tried to preserve. Education was still valued very much by the elected government and so our schools were taken care of. The brick was all original and tended to yearly, with no chipped paint in the classrooms and no broken windows. The grounds however were not considered essential and so the vegetation that had survived in this climate was kind of wild.

Joel, Katie, and I took our seats as the rest of the classroom filed in. Professor Abner seemed to treat the stories he told with reverence, as though they were more than just that. He began his lecture on the ways our ancestors used to track animals and why those

Ashley Kaplan

practices were so important for us in today's world. I couldn't pay attention to him, being so exhausted from my restless night; the nightmares have kept me up. I didn't notice that I was beginning to fall asleep.

"How did you get here?"

I could hear the woman's voice but it was muffled, as though she spoke to me underwater.

"Get here?" I said groggily.

"You're not supposed to be here."

"Where?" What are you talking about?" Everything was dark and murky and I felt weighed down by pressure as though I was underwater too. "Where am I?"

"You shouldn't be here, even if you are one of ours."

"One of who? what is going on?"

"You are not like the rest. You can return it."

"It?" I asked, confused.

"It's mine, you must return it to me."

"I didn't take anything, I don't know what you're talking about." I began to shout, frustrated with her accusations.

"Return what is mine before the Infernals get you too."

"Infernals?" the word was barely out of my mouth when I felt a tugging, like a tether attached to my belly button. I gasped as the sharp movement sucked me out of wherever I was.

"Hey, wake up!" Katie was shaking me. "Ari, come on, class is over."

I blinked my eyes open, the light too bright and sharp. "Oh no," I groaned. "Did Abner see?"

Katie and Joel exchanged nervous glances; Professor Abner was looking right at me with a glare that said he wasn't impressed. I threw my head back and slumped in my seat. *Great*, I thought, *a lecture after my lecture was exactly what I need.*

Ashley Kaplan

Katie smiled at me sympathetically. "Listen I have to get to my next class but cheer up, maybe go home and get some sleep."

"Yeah, what she said," Joel agreed. "You look like—"

"Don't," I put my hand up to stop him. "Finish that sentence and you're a dead man."

"And that's my cue, ladies and gentlemen." He jumped up out of his seat and bowed to us theatrically. "See you guys for lunch."

"You gonna be ok?" Katie asked, giving my arm an encouraging squeeze.

"Peachy," I said with a thumbs-up. "Go, I'll see you later."

I waved her off and dragged my feet over to Professor Abner, smiling apologetically at his raised brow.

"Forgive me, I did not realize my lecture would be so boring."

"Sorry Professor, I didn't get much sleep last night."

"Ari, while I understand that you may not find all this information entertaining there is still a great deal you could learn from it."

Here comes the lecture. "I know, I'm sorry, I had these freaky monster dreams—"

"Monster?"

"—and then the coffee this morning I thought would for sure give me a boost—"

"What sort of dream?"

"—but then the nap dream was bizarre too and maybe it's something I'm eating? Can food give you weird dreams? Oh god, I hope it's not the coffee."

"Ari," he stopped me. "Calm down, perhaps it would be best if you went home and got some rest."

I was too tired to argue with him. I was zoning out. "Katie said the same thing."

"Yes, well very wise that Katie," he said, ushering me out. "Go home and I'll speak with you later."

I nodded and waved to him as I walked out of his classroom. I was too tired to sit through my classes today. Maybe if I got some rest, I would feel refreshed. I felt like I had used up all of my energy and there was none left to spare.

As I walked through the university grounds, my hands clutching the straps of my backpack, I took a deep breath. Once I got some rest I would feel better and I hoped there would be no

Ashley Kaplan

more nightmares. I was looking forward to nothing but kittens and puppies in my dreams. The sun was beating down on me as I slipped into the empty walkway between two of the buildings. It was a shortcut off campus to get to my apartment. Even though the day was humid, I was suddenly accosted by a penetrating cold. Shivers ran down my spine and I slowed to a stop and raised my arm, looking at the goosebumps spreading across it. I couldn't explain where the cold was coming from. Once I stopped I was able to hear it – a low hum behind me, almost like panting. My instincts told me not to turn around but I had to know what it was. Who it was. Had they been following me last night as well?

I turned ever so slightly and my eyes grew wider in disbelief.

"What the hell...?" I breathed out.

Standing before me was what looked like a man but his face... there was something wrong with it. The eyes were black as night with a nose that looked more like a dog snout. Foam was gathered around the corners of the mouth. I could see—*oh god was that a mouth full of fangs?*

Panting with its entire body, like an animal. Its arms were muscular and the skin from the forearms down was as black as ink. Its fingers ended in claws and it stood on human legs but from the knee down they looked like dog paws, with a claw at the heel. I heard a growl from the back of the creatures throat and its mouth twisted into a grotesque smile.

Run, idiot! Get out of here!

I snapped myself out of the shock just long enough to spin around and run like my life depended on it. Looking at that thing, I realized that it probably did. My heart was in my throat; I heard it bound after me but I was a strong runner. *Maybe I can outrun it.* Just as quickly as I thought that, its claws tore into my backpack and yanked me down onto my backside. I landed with a wince and looked up. The creature raised its claws again but my instincts kicked in and I slipped one arm out of the strap of my backpack and rolled. As its claws came down and got caught in the material, it yanked, and I was able to pull my other arm free, the movement causing the creature to stumble backward.

Using that momentum I raised my leg and kicked it straight in the chest, sending the thing tumbling onto its back, then I turned to run again. This time it was quicker. The creature jumped and somehow flew over my head, landed in front of me, and with one flick of the arm sent me flying against a garbage can. I hit the metal with a loud clunk and fell to the ground on all fours as it came to stand over me. Seeming to grow larger and taller as it panted even harder. I didn't know what to do. The creature was faster than me, stronger too. I lowered my head and raised my arm in a vain attempt to shield myself from the attack...

But nothing happened.

Ashley Kaplan

"Get away from her!"

The creature stopped and turned. Professor Abner was standing there, legs spread, a determined look on his face and, if I was seeing this right, a sword in his hand.

"Get away from the girl."

The thing tore through the air like a wild animal, running at the professor, but Abner didn't move. Didn't even flinch. Instead, I watched in amazement as he sidestepped the attack and swung the sword back, slicing the creature's right arm off at the elbow. Abner turned to face the thing as it let out a blood-curdling screech that sounded like a dozen voices crying in unison. The blood pouring from its wound was jet black. It looked at Abner with hatred in its eyes, and back at me, the intended prey. Abner took a step to the side to shield me from its vision.

"Look at me. I'm the one you should worry about."

The creature opened its mouth wider than it should have been able to and screamed at Abner before lunging forward again. Abner let the beast take him down to the ground and as he landed, he drove the sword through his stomach with full force.

The thing fell off him and clutched the sword with his remaining hand. It writhed on the floor like a worm, screaming as its body slowly began to steam. It melted into an inky black puddle and soon there was nothing but a sword laying on the ground in its place. Professor Abner picked up his sword, wiped the hilt, and sheathed it. He turned to me, sitting wide-eyed on the ground.

"Arianna?" he said stepping forward. "Ari, are you alright? Did it hurt you?"

The shock finally wearing off, I let out the scream I had been holding in from the moment I saw the creature. Abner was by my side in moments, grabbing me by the shoulders and helping me up.

I was shaking, balling my hands into fists. I shuddered, trying to physically erase the memory.

"Did you see that?!" I shouted. "Oh my god, I've lost my mind. I'm having a nervous breakdown."

"You are not crazy, Ari."

"Are you telling me that was real? And you! How did you...? No. No, this is impossible."

"Arianna calm down," he said grabbing me by the shoulders again. "I promise to explain everything but right now we have to go. Now that they have your scent there will be more of them coming, do you understand me?"

I swallowed hard and nodded. "Okay."

"Right then, let's go, quickly."

Ashley Kaplan

I followed Professor Abner to where his car was still running. I got in the front, pulling my legs to my chest and watching the road disappear behind me as Abner sped off.

He had his phone in his hands within seconds. "Orion, I need an extraction immediately. My charge has been made, I'm bringing her in."

I couldn't hear the voice on the other end but I saw Abner's brow furrow as he spun the wheel sharply, turning the car around.

"Understood, I'm on my way there now." He hung up.

"Hey Abner, as much as I love a good mystery, and you know this is a GREAT one – really, a gold medal on the whole mystery thing here – but do you want to clue me in on what the hell is going on?!" I shouted the last part.

Abner was speeding down side streets and driving like a mad man. "I can't get into all of it right now. There's another Gifted that needs our help."

The word echoed through my head.

"Gifted?"

"Rare and unique individuals, like yourself. That thing that was after you, it's called an Infernal. And where there's one..."

I thought back to Professor Abner's lectures and to the story that I read Murphy last night. The Gifted... the Zodiacs... the pieces were coming together in my head.

"What did it want?"

"It was hunting you. Your blood emanates a certain smell to them. It must have been watching for a while."

"Last night, I felt... I don't know."

"Cold. They can't abide the heat. Any time an Infernal is around the air turns to ice."

My mind was spinning. How could this be real? It couldn't be real. I had to get a grip, fast, because it seemed that we weren't out of the woods just yet. Abner skidded the car to a halt before a grey alleyway. There was a manhole at its entrance and the steam it let out made the whole scene that much more foreboding.

"Stay here," he commanded and jumped out.

I watched him disappear into the alley and shut my eyes. I was NOT going to follow him, no way! I didn't much feel like a hero after the way I'd handled the first Infernal I'd ever seen. That had only been minutes ago and I was not eager to go face another one just yet. *But what if Abner needs help?* I thought. *There could be another kid freaking out over there.* I couldn't just let Murphy become an orphan because I was a coward.

"Damn it!" I cursed as I swung the door open and hopped out after Professor Abner.

Ashley Kaplan

As I stepped closer, the steam obscured my view. I waved my hand in front of my face, hearing the grunting sounds of a fight before the air cleared and I saw them. Abner was facing off against another Infernal, sword in hand, stretched out across him in a defensive posture. The Infernal stared him down, clicking its back claws on the ground. I gasped and they both turned to me. The Infernal circled its head in a snake-like motion as though it was smelling me. Its eyes widened and I could tell immediately... it knew.

Whatever they thought I was, the Infernal knew it.

"Ari, get the boy out of here!" Abner shouted "Now!"

He lunged forward and pushed the creature down. They both tumbled to the ground and rolled.

My eyes searched the alley until I saw the boy, sitting against the wall, holding onto his right side. He had black boots and faded, loose jeans, and a black V-neck t-shirt. His dark hair went down to his shoulders and wisps of it fell over his eyes. I could see him wincing and I jumped into action. Running over to him, I noticed the blood. He had a gash along his ribs that looked pretty bad.

"Can you walk?" I asked.

He tried to sit up and winced, sucking in a deep breath. "I'm ok. I can walk."

"Ok, good. Everything is going to be alright," I told him in a confident tone I didn't feel. I put an arm under his and helped him to his feet. He stumbled for a moment but then regained his footing.

"Right around that corner is a red car," I said. "There's a phone. Find the last number dialed and ask for help."

"I'm not leaving," he said through gritted teeth. "I can't just leave that thing loose."

"We don't have time for this." I turned my back on him, gearing up to fight. "Get out of here."

"Wait, What are you doing?"

"I'm going to be the distraction."

I ran towards Abner. The Infernal had him pinned down and Abner was just managing to hold it off with the sword, but it was coming down on him.

"Hey ugly!" I yelled and the thing turned to me, saliva drooling from its mouth. "Wow, you actually turned around. Do all of you answer to that or are you just extremely self-aware of... all... of this?" I gestured with my hands over the length of its body.

"Ari, get out of here!" Abner shouted, but I could see the creature loosen its hold. It could smell me now.

Ashley Kaplan

"You know what I am?" I asked it, digging my feet in and raising my arms in a defensive stance. "Come and get me then."

I don't know what possessed me to do it. I hoped that I could give Abner just a little space so he could go on the attack. I had trained for years but never had to fight someone in a real life situation. The sessions were always controlled. I guess I was about to find out what all that training was for.

The Infernal wasn't as dumb as I hoped. It caught Abner's blade in its claws and spun it out of his grip, then backhanded him across the face, knocking Abner down to the ground. The sword went flying and skid just a few feet away from me. My eyes darted towards it and then back at the Infernal. I didn't think I would make it to the sword before it made it to me. By the look on its face, the creature knew it too, but I had to try.

I ran towards the sword and the Infernal ran after me. I got low to the ground and rolled forward, landing on my knees as my fingers gripped the blade. The Infernal was almost on top of me when he was tackled to the ground. It was that guy, the one we came to save. The Infernal squirmed like a worm and then shot up to its feet. The guy stood to face him, his fists at his sides, his shirt drenched in blood. I tightened my grip on the sword and closed the gap between us. The stranger and I faced the Infernal.

"I thought you were here to rescue *me,* not the other way around," he said sarcastically.

"Yeah well, what can I say? It's my first day."

"Great."

The Infernal looked between us as though trying to decide who to go for. It was an easy pick for it – go for the wounded one, easier to subdue. It jumped into the air and kicked me down, snatching the guy as it went. I pushed off the pavement to my feet and saw the Infernal drag his kicking victim. My arm pulled back and I flung the sword full force at the creature. I thought I felt a burst of air push the sword forward on a straight axis until it dug itself with a whoosh into the Infernal's chest. The creatures eyes bugged out as it clutched at the sword, desperately trying to pull it out, but it was too late. TheInfernal blew up like a black water balloon, splashing our feet.

I bent over, leaning my hands on my knees, catching my breath. When I looked back up I could see Professor Abner standing in the alley. His eyes met mine and If I didn't know any better, I'd say that he looked proud. He retrieved the sword and stopped over the guy who still lay on the floor.

"We have to get that wound tended to," Abner said. "What's your name?"

The stranger propped himself up on his elbows, I could tell that the movement pained him. "Is that thing dead?"

"It's dead." Professor Abner assured him.

The stranger propped himself up on his elbows, I could tell that the movement pained him. "Is that thing dead?"

"It's dead." Professor Abner assured him.

The stranger threw his head back and closed his eyes. I could see the relief wash over him even as his body tensed in pain. I wondered how long that thing had been chasing him. Professor Abner bent down to his eye level. "We have to get out of here, before any more of them show up," he said calmly.

The stranger opened his eyes and nodded. Abner hooked an arm under him and helped the guy to his feet; the two limped over to me.

"I am Professor Abner, this is—"

"Ari, yeah, I heard. I'm Damien."

Ashley Kaplan

Pisces
Aries
Taurus
Gemini
Cancer
Leo
Virgo
Libra
Scorpio
Sagittarius
Capricorn
Aquarius

Stories

I glanced over my shoulder at Damien. He had been laying in the back seat with his eyes closed ever since we fled the city. Dirt and sand flanked either side of the long, paved road, cutting through the desert. He opened his bright blue eyes and peered into mine.

"What?" he asked, just as we hit a bump. He flinched as it tossed him upwards.

"Abner, we need to get him to help soon. He's not looking too good."

"Gee, thanks."

"It's not far now, nearly there," Abner said in his relaxed, patient, way.

"Yeah, Professor Abner, was it? I have a few questions about the *where?*" Damien struggled to sit.

"Now that we're not running for our lives, I'd also like an explanation," I agreed.

Abner respired, "we're going to Astro City. It's got wards against the Infernals. They won't be able to track us there."

"Astro?" I had trouble recalling the name. "I've never heard of a place like that."

"The government believes it's a military town that was evacuated many years ago due to toxic exposure from . Of course, it has always been Astro. No such military city exists."

Damien passed a sidelong glace over Abner, narrowing his gaze. "Nobody ever came to investigate?"

"Oh, people have come now and again, but with the Zodiac's gifts, they are easy to manipulate into believing what we need them to."

Damien snorted. "This is ridiculous."

"Let me put it to you this way. You've heard the story of the Zodiacs back in ancient times?"

"The so-called gods?" Damien rolled his eyes.

Professor Abner chanced a look at me, "those legends I teach in class, the ones that seemed impossible, they're all true. The Zodiacs walked among us many years ago. Bestowing a gift to mortals born under their signs, ones deemed to be *true heroes*. A speck of their godly power. We call those people the *Gifted*. They passed these powers down from one generation to the next. Some Gifted have been able to tap into their powers since birth, then there are those whose gifts lay dormant. Sometimes never surfacing."

I glanced down at my hands, curling my fingers into my palms and stretching them again. Something happened to me in that alleyway, I could feel the power surging from within. As terrified as I felt, I knew Abner was telling the truth.

"How did you know? About Damien and me?" I asked. "How did you know?"

Abner's continence wavered, but he kept his eyes on the road. "We've always known about you. We know where every legacy is. That is what we call the children of the Gifted. We provide each legacy with a guardian to watch over them until such a time as they are needed. To protect you from the Infernals, or to explain, should your powers awaken."

My world shattered, leaving nothing *real* behind. *If Abner wasn't who he claimed to be, was anyone in my life real? Genuine?*

"So, one of my parents was Gifted," I said to myself. "You knew," I whispered, my face betraying me. I felt disturbed, like I was a science experiment. "This whole time..."

"This is a joke, right?" Damien snorted in derision, "don't tell me you believe this guy?"

I turned to him. "That's how you were able to tackle the Infernal. You're hurt. There's no way you should have been able to do that."

"It was adrenaline," Damien said unconvincingly.

"No, it wasn't! Just like the sword I threw flying straight at that thing. You felt it too. Well... didn't you?" I stared at him, daring him to lie to me.

Ashley Kaplan

Damien didn't flinch. He furrowed his brow stubbornly but didn't say a word. Looking into his eyes, I knew he felt what I had. *What I was still reeling from.*

"We're here," Abner interrupted my thoughts, "I'll answer all your questions as soon as we get that wound looked at."

Damien and I strained to see the city through the windows.

"Whoa," we both breathed out simultaneously in wonder.

We had driven through the desert to the base of the mountain. Tucked right into its curve was Astro City, surrounded by a white stone wall that went on for miles. Its height was impressive and at its entry, an arch tapered to a sharp peak. Beyond the wall I could see into the center of the city where a collection of golden domed roofs gleamed. One structure stood taller than the rest. There were windows along its walls and open walkways between the higher levels. Once we drove through the archway, I had to open my window, as though it would somehow make the vision more real to me.

There was so much greenery surrounding me, trees lining the streets. Robust and healthy vines grew from the ground and clung tightly to the walls of homes and buildings. They seemed to have been built years ago, the architecture speaking to the age of the city. We drove past beautifully designed cream stone water fountains. I hadn't seen one of those in my lifetime, not one that was working. Water was not to be wasted like that. But here? Everything flourished, given the breath of life from the abundance of water they seemed to have. Nobody paid any attention to us, but I couldn't help be riveted by them.

"Abner h-how?" I whispered.

Even before I heard his answer, we came into direct view of the domed building. Around me the air buzzed with something; a power akin to mine. I glanced at Damien, and I could sense he felt the same thing. Abner stopped the carat the entryway and I stepped out breathless. Walking up to the two wooden doors of the entrance, I noticed there were carvings all along their front. As I placed my hand on the wood, I let my fingers glide across the grooves until I realized what I was looking at. The star constellations that made up the Zodiac signs. Something in my body called from within. Perhaps it was the aimless foster kid in me, or maybe it was something deeper and older than I could understand.

Once those doors swung open, it swept away Damien and I into Professor Abner's world. Everything was bright inside the fortress, the white walls and floors glowing under the sunlight cascading through the many windows. The building's architecture was as old as the rest of the city, which made me wonder just how long it had stood there. Abner grabbed Damien under the arm and directed him where to go.

"Hey man, watch it."

Abner walked with a purpose, and we could only follow. To our right, I heard quick footsteps and suddenly someone else flanked us.

"Professor, glad to see you came out alright," the stranger said.

"Hello Jonah," Abner spoke, continuing his stride, "as you can see, we made it out, but we need a medic."

"On site and ready for you, sir," Jonah said.

"And my son?" Abner asked.

Jonah grinned happily, "little dude was picked up and is settling in just fine, waiting for you."

I could see the tension ease from Abner's shoulders when he heard Murphy was safe.

"Professor, what about Phillips?"

Abner lowered his head and sighed. "haven't had that conversation yet. Please, have Calypso meet us in the war room."

"You got it, sir." As he turned on his heels to leave, his eye caught mine. He grinned and winked at me before sprinting off.

Abner burst through another door, into what was an infirmary, still holding on to Damien. Cots lined one wall and medical equipment on the other. Through glass doors, a modern feature for this building, I could see a closed-off lab. Presumably where the doctor could work. A man was sitting at that table now. He had a smooth-shaven face and head. He seemed to be in his mid-forties, wearing a scowl as he studied something I couldn't see. Once he heard our intrusion, he jumped to his feet and walked out of his office, immediately helping Damien onto a cot.

"Professor Abner, never with a shortage of patients for me," he said sarcastically.

"An Infernal attacked him."

"Yes, yes, they are always attacked by something." The doctor said patiently, lifting Damien's shirt to inspect the wound.

"Hey buddy," Damien smacked his hands away, "you want to take me to dinner first?"

The doctor paused and raised a brow. "Young man, please spare me the theatrics. You are hurt. I am a doctor. Let's go on with our intended roles for the moment."

Damien seemed apprehensive, but luckily better judgment won out as he lifted his shirt for the doctor.

"Whatever."

"Right," the doctor said as he felt around the wound, "I am Dr. Levine and you will need stitches."

"Like hell!"

The doctor threw his hands up in the air, "Abner, please instill some sense into this young man —"

"For the love of..." I snapped, "will you just let him patch you up? There are more important things to get to."

Damien glared at the doctor, but it was Abner's soft and steady voice that broke through.

"Um, yes, perhaps Arianna and I should step out and give you some privacy. I suspect you have a lot more questions, Damien? It would be a lot easier to answer them after you've been looked at."

Damien narrowed his eyes.

"We will leave you to it then," Abner said, taking that as a sign of surrender as he ushered me out. I heard the doctor instruct Damien to remove his torn and bloodstained shirt, and glanced back at him. I couldn't help but appreciate his physique under that shirt. By the looks of him, Damien took care of-

"Oh, ow," I said with a wince as I walked right into the door.

"Gods, are you alright?" Abner asked, grabbing hold of the door and pulling it open for me.

My cheeks burned. "I, yes." Flustered, I collected myself. "I'm good, um, fine, thanks."

I wasn't sure, but I thought I might have heard Damien chuckle behind me.

Ashley Kaplan

I followed Abner down the strange halls of the compound in silence. I wasn't sure what to say to him, still acclimating to my new situation. Abner knew about me this whole time, and I still had so many questions for him. I realized, unlike the people outside, the ones here had a very specific purpose. This was obviously a military base, which begged the question... What war were they fighting? And against who? Based on my earlier experience, I wasn't sure I wanted to know the answer.

Abner led me through a set of doors into a room that seemed to be a meeting space. In the center sat a large round table, a depiction of the world map drawn on it, and several wooden chairs surrounding it. Those were the only wood items in the room. The rest was a harsh metal contrasting the warm, round furniture. Several computers were running across the room, some showing surveillance. The walls featured rows of bookshelves with old, leather-bound books. I wasn't much of a reader, but even *I* was impressed by their seeming importance. My gaze drifted upwards to the ceiling painted a stark, dark blue to mirror the night sky. Splashes across it reflected a smattering of stars, and among them were the Zodiac constellations. Perfectly mapped out.

There was a girl who seemed to be my age, or maybe a couple of years older, bent over a computer watching a surveillance video. Her black, pin-straight hair with wisps of bright pink was a contrast to her fair skin. She had outlined her angular brown eyes with black eyeliner, but wore no other makeup. The black t-shirt she wore hung loosely compared to her skin-tight, black pants and black boots. She looked fierce and sexy, it made me feel instantly self-conscious. Once she noticed us, she smiled brightly and met us at the round table.

"You finally made it. I was beginning to worry."

"We ran into some trouble but as you can see, we managed to make it out alright," Abner answered.

"Any news on Phillips?" she asked. For the second time in twenty minutes I wondered, who is Philips?

Abner sighed, "I'm afraid only his charge can answer that question at the moment. Has Orion been successful?"

The girl shrugged. "He's out with a team. Still trying to track down any leads, but so far, it seems those were the only two Infernals in the area."

Abner furrowed his brow. "It's rather peculiar that there should be two attacks in one day. They seem to be speeding up their search."

"What does that mean?" she asked warily.

"Nothing good, I'm afraid," he answered with a sigh. "Well, in any event, Calypso, I'd like you to meet Arianna March. Ari, this is Calypso. She oversees surveillance here."

Calypso smiled warmly at me. "Welcome to Astro City Abner has said so many wonderful things about you."

I cocked my head at Abner, the comment driving deeper than the fact he had known about me all along. *Other people here had known more about me than I did myself.* I couldn't believe that he kept this enormous secret hidden from me. My stomach began knotting again.

"I wish I could say the same, but it's nice to meet you either way."

Calypso's smile faltered.

Abner cleared his throat. "Do you have footage of the campus grounds on there?"

"Yeah, have a look," she gestured, and they walked away, leaving me standing and gawking. I walked over to the bookshelves and browsed through the titles. They were all legends about the Zodiacs. Some, centered on magics, and others over rituals. One book read *Creatures of the Cursed*, and seeing the word in plural gave me pause. Did the word imply many or of several varieties? I didn't want to imagine the latter, although the former made me just as sick. I stepped away and headed back to the table before my head exploded.

Just then, the doors burst open, and Damien walked in wearing a new shirt. He looked around the room and, if I wasn't mistaken; he seemed annoyed.

"Ah, Mr. Bardin," Professor Abner welcomed, "all patched up?"

"Yeah, the Doc gave me a once over then had someone bring me here."

"Very good, please have a seat," Abner gestured for both of us to sit with him, and Calypso. Damien shot me a look, and I shrugged. We obliged, Damien was likely as exhausted as I.

"I'd like you to meet Calypso," Abner said. "This is Damien Bardin, Phillips's charge."

Calypso's eyes widened. "Have you seen him?"

"Who the hell are you talking about?"

Abner narrowed his eyes as though he were seeing Damien for the first time. "Damien, what exactly do you remember before today?"

I could see it plainly on Damien's face. The uncertainty, the doubt, and suddenly all his anger made sense. He wasn't giving us an attitude because he didn't trust strangers. He was watchful because he didn't trust anyone; he didn't remember anyone.

"Nothing, alright?" he sighed. "I woke up in an alleyway behind a mechanic's shop. I had a gash on my head that was bleeding and there was a" he faltered, "there was a guy on the ground." Damien paused, his jaw clenching as he continued. "I went over to him, but it was too late. He was gone. That's when I heard *that thing* jump out at me. I don't know how I knocked it out and I have no idea who the guy was. I only knew my name from an ID in my wallet. I ran but that thing caught up to me. That's when you guys showed up."

Calypso closed her eyes and bowed her head. "Oh Phillips, you deserved better."

I watched as Professor Abner took a moment to compose himself before he finally spoke. "Have you told the doctor about your memory loss?"

Damien nodded. "He said it was likely a result of a concussion and that it will come back to me." He seemed resentful of himself for forgetting. Like it was his fault.

"Very well," Abner continued. "There is no easy way to say this, but Owen Phillips was your Guardian. Yours and your brothers'."

"Brother?" Damien echoed.

"Yes, more precisely, your twin brother. Theron. You two owned the mechanic's shop, along with Owen. I understand your powers showed quite early, as you were able to bounce them off your brother and the other way around. In case you were wondering, you have the Gift of Gemini."

Damien slumped back in his chair. "This is all just a little too wild for me."

Calypso offered a reassuring smile. "Hey man, you're lucky. Although our powers get passed down the bloodline, the Gemini gift only manifests in sets of twins."

Abner nodded. "The combination makes it fairly rare to have this gift."

"This is a lot of information to take in one day," I said, feeling overwhelmed.

Damien looked stoic, however, "and my brother, do you know what happened to him?"

"We were hoping you could tell us," Abner bowed his head and rubbed the bridge of his nose, "now we can only wait on Orion for word. He's out scouting the area." He raised his head again and looked to me next, "as for you Ari, you have inherited the gift of Aquarius. An air sign, which is why you could manipulate the air around you, if a bit crudely," he shrugged, "but with ease."

"Do you know which one of my parents was" I couldn't finish the sentence; it didn't seem real.

"Your mother," he breathed.

"Did they" I swallowed, forcing the question I feared, "did the Infernals"

"No," Abner spared me, "it was a car accident, as you were told."

"Why didn't you bring us here sooner?" I asked.

Professor Abner sighed. "We try not to interfere with our charge's lives unless we have to. You see, The Council of Twelve protect the Gifted. Centuries ago, they decided they should appoint a Guardian to each legacy. As I've told you, it's what we call the children of the Gifted. If the legacy's power manifest, then we intervene. Otherwise, we are there merely to observe and guard. Some Legacies go on for generations not tapping into their power before one from their bloodline becomes Gifted."

Damien sat up. "And those who suddenly find themselves chock-full of Gifted Zodiac steroids get what?"

I couldn't blame him for his anger. How could these people make such monumental decisions for us?

"Well, they are brought here to live alongside the other Gifted. Most of them train to become Astral Warriors, to protect other legacies and humanity against the Infernals and other such creatures."

"You want us to fight?" I asked, astonished.

"You must understand, Arianna, the Gifted were hand chosen by the gods. It is your birthright," Abner tried to explain.

"Our birthright?" I laughed humourlessly. "Death and fear? Some birthright."

"We didn't do this to you, Ari," said Calypso. "The Zodiacs *chose* your bloodline. Like it or not, you're one of us. You don't belong in that other world; you are a part of something so much bigger."

I understood nothing about their world, but I felt like my brain couldn't handle much more nor could my body.

"What about the people here?" Damien asked. "Is everyone in this city like us?"

"No, actually. Most of the people here are families of the Gifted individuals. Others are guardians, like me, and their families as well. There are a few legacies in the city, others scattered around the world. We know of forty bloodlines in existence that carry the Zodiac's gift."

"Forty?" I asked incredulously.

Calypso nodded, "we lost track of a few bloodlines though over time, but only a handful. Presumably, they are dead, but we don't know that for sure."

"So out of those forty legacies, how many became Gifted?" asked Damien.

"Including you two?" Calypso asked, "twenty-five right now."

"This is probably all I can handle for today," I said, rubbing my temples to relieve what might be the beginning of a headache.

Abner straightened. "Yes, I should say you two have had quite the day. Calypso, please find some rooms for these two to get settled? Until we can make more permanent arrangements. I believe some rest is in order."

"There is still one pretty big question you haven't answered yet," Damien said. "Why were those Infernals after us to begin with?"

Damien asked what should have been my first question. Why did these things want us dead? I had a feeling we would not like this answer any better.

"If you might recall," Abner began, "the legends mention the Cursed One, a being whose jealousy of the Gifted took over them. Her name is Amelia, but where she got her powers is still a mystery to us. She commands the Infernals and for centuries, since she has gained her power, her sole mission has been to destroy the humans most dear to the Zodiacs."

"Us Gifted represent everything she couldn't have," Calypso added. "The very power the gods denied her."

"Once Amelia unleashed the Infernals, they wreaked havoc on humanity in their search for the Gifted. Finally, these powered individuals could no longer ignore the devastation and formed the Council of Twelve. They organized the Gifted and together formed the Astral Army. Warriors dedicated to protecting humanity."

"It was this very war that forced the Zodiacs to retreat," Calypso said with sadness, maybe even guilt. "Once unleashed on the world the Infernals never stopped their devastation. Our ancestors managed to fight them off and our people continue to track them and protect humanity from their brutal assaults."

"Whatever dark hole Amelia opened to let the Infernals and their kin out, the Astral Warriors are dedicated to protecting humanity from such beasts. Meanwhile Amelia has not abandoned her efforts to seek out and destroy all that is left of the Zodiac's legacy. As long as your kind exists, she will stop at nothing to wipe out the Legacy bloodlines."

Damien and I must have looked like deer in headlights because they left us speechless.

"You know what? I don't think I want to know anymore," I said.

To my everlasting relief, Damien kept his mouth shut and asked no more questions. Calypso only paused a moment and then nodded, walking past us to the door and holding it

Ashley Kaplan

open in waiting. Unsure what else waited beyond that door, I wasn't overly eager to find out.

Aries
Taurus
Gemini
Cancer
Leo
Virgo
Libra
Scorpio
Sagittarius
Capricorn
Aquarius
Pisces

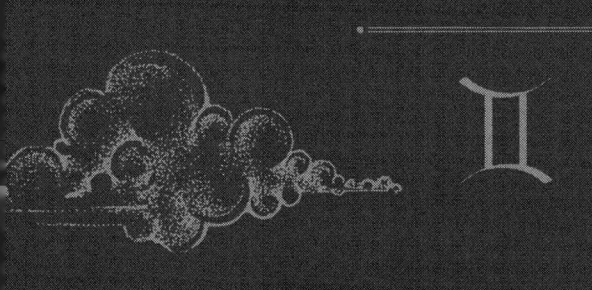

Astro

We trailed behind Calypso. I wasn't sure about Damien but I'd felt the shift inside me and if the Infernals could find me that way, I knew there was no going back. Not right now anyway, not without putting my friends in danger. Calypso was talking as we walked, pointing out different areas of the base that we might find of interest.

The brightness of the base along with its wide halls and high ceilings made the place feel like a palace. Calypso walked us past a courtyard that was fairly large with a brick pathway and a water fountain in its center. On either side of the path were manicured hedges and trees, as well as short, black lamp posts.

"Calypso," I began hesitantly, "how is it that you guys have so much water to use?"

"It comes from our powers," she explained. "We all have a hand in keeping the city going but our gifts can help us control water and pull it right from the ground. The water helps our crops grow as well our trees and grass. We are blessed."

"So what's your deal?" Damien asked her. "Or what's your gift, I should say?"

Calypso grinned and turned her wrist as she walked, a small spark igniting in her palm.

"I have the Gift of Leo, of fire and light." She waved her hand and the spark vanished.

"Wow, that's unbelievable," I said. "And this place, I've never seen an army base like this before"

"This isn't just a base, Ari. We live here. All of us Gifted who needed refuge live in Astro City. It's the only place we are assured of safety."

"When did you get here?" I asked her.

"Oh I was born here," she said happily. "Look I'm sure this whole world is kind of a shock to you. Soon enough you'll run into things you probably never thought existed."

"Why am I not loving the sound of that?" Damien grunted.

"Like what?" I asked.

"Like witches and seers, or mythic animals… the minotaurs run their game in the mountain but they seem worse than they are. If you look closely over the horizon, you might be able to catch the glimpse of a phoenix. They are drawn to our power."

Before I had a chance to respond something flew at me and attached itself to my waist. I was momentarily knocked off balance but caught myself. I looked down to see Murphy's bright, smiling face as he hugged me.

"You're here!" he shouted excitedly.

"Hey Murph," I said and squeezed him tight. "I heard you were around here somewhere."

"So," he said as he stepped away, hands on hips with a smug smile, "told you it was all real."

I blinked in surprise and couldn't help the laugh that escaped me. Here I was with my whole world turned upside down and Murphy was gloating in a way only a child could. *This must seem like such a grand adventure to him,* I thought.

I smiled at him. "You sure did. I'm still deciding if that's a good thing."

Murphy turned to Damien and looked him up and down. "Who're you?"

Damien raised an eyebrow. "What's it to you, kid?"

"My dad runs the place," he said matter-of-factly, "so I kind of know everyone."

"Is that right?" Damien might have tried looking stern but I could see the amusement in his eyes. It made him somehow seem softer. "Knowing my name isn't the same as knowing me," he said.

Murphy thought that over for a moment. "Ok, yeah. I guess that's true."

"But I just got here," Damien shrugged, "so you'll get your chance to get to know me. I'm Damien."

Murphy seemed satisfied with that and turned to Calypso. "Is my dad here yet?"

"You bet. He's in the war room so make sure you knock first." She winked at him and offered a fist. Murphy bumped it and waved to us as he ran off.

"Gotta find dad, see you later," he called out.

"You know that kid?" Damien asked me, amused.

"I babysit occasionally," I offered lamely.

We fell back into step with Calypso as she took us to another set of rooms, one labeled TR1. It was very clear that this room, and others like it, were used for training.

There were mats on the floor, a desk, and a chair off to one side with mirrors along one wall. The other wall sported weapons behind clear locked doors along with other equipment.

"This is Training Room 1, where you will come tomorrow to test your skills and where we can see what we have to work with."

"Now we're talking," Damien said as he eyed the weapons.

"Come on," Calypso grinned, "let's get you settled in your rooms."

We followed her up a flight of stairs and then another to the third floor where there were rows of single rooms.

"Most of the Gifted move into the city once they have finished their training but some remain here on site with us," she offered.

Our rooms were just a few doors apart from each other. "Have a good night you two. You can relax, you're safe now."

"Wait," I stopped her. "Hold on. This is great, and I appreciate you guys taking us in for tonight, but how long do we have to stay here?"

"Excuse me?"

"When can we go home?"

Calypso looked warily at me and then at Damien and hesitantly replied, "We can discuss that with Abner tomorrow. For now, you should get some rest."

With those parting words, she walked away, and I couldn't help but watch her. Her walk was sure and confident, not just as someone who knew where she was going but as someone who knew herself. Something I could no longer say was true for me.

I took a deep breath and awkwardly waved goodbye to Damien as I stepped into my room and locked the door behind me. The room was a fair size, with beautiful arched windows looking out over the grounds. There was one bed in the center with a nightstand on each side, two lamps, and a desk and chair on the other side of the room. There was a closet as well but of course, it was empty. I dragged my weary body over to the bed and fell on top of it in a heap. Maybe now I could finally get some rest.

After the day I'd had, I thought maybe now I could finally get some sleep but as I lay in the bed sleep never came. It was too early; I was too restless with so much to think about. Muttering under my breath I decided to take a walk around the grounds. I wasn't sure where I was going, just that I needed to get out, and somehow I ended up in the training hall. Tomorrow I was to report to TR1 and I found myself drawn to it now. I walked into the dark room with only a small backlight offering some visibility. Tomorrow I was going to start training here; tomorrow my new life was supposed to begin. Had I resigned myself to it already? *But how can I not? Now that I've seen what's out there?* I thought. How was I supposed to protect myself?

"It's a bit overwhelming isn't it?" Professor Abner asked, coming behind me. He stopped at the table in front of the mats and sat on the edge of it, crossing his arms over his chest.

"What?" I asked, not daring to look at him. "The whole finding out I have super powers gifted by the gods? No, it's... just another Tuesday night" I joked lamely.

"I'm sorry you had to find out this way," he sighed.

"Were you ever going to tell me?" I asked quietly, looking Professor Abner dead in the eyes. I needed a reason, an explanation for all of this.

"It was never my intention to keep this from you, Ari."

"You let me get lost in the system. I was just another foster kid who could have ended up anywhere."

"That would have never happened. I made sure that anywhere you ended up they understood it was imperative to keep you safe."

"Made sure how?" I asked, my thoughts went to Katie and her amazing parents.

"Arianna... as your Guardian I had to make sure you would be safe. I offered these families the tools to help prepare you for this life."

I felt breathless, like the wind had been knocked out of me in one fell swoop. I saw all of my memories crashing around me, no longer sure of what was real and what wasn't. The martial arts lessons, self-defense classes, boxing. Abner had made sure that I was training even then; he was grooming me for this life.

"How could you?" I whispered, "I trusted you."

"You have the potential to do great things and as your Guardian it is my job to prepare you to use your Gift. I know a thing or two about power, Ari, and it can be destructive. I wanted you to have a chance at a normal life. To see what being a regular human was like. To feel their hopes, their pain, their dreams."

"This whole time I was a walking target. Why did you let me believe I could have a normal life?" I asked, tears burning behind my eyes. "So that it would hurt more when you ripped me out of it?"

"So that when the time came, you could be a true hero. One who was worthy of your gift. A hero is not defined by their power but by how they wield it. Through kindness, they show the inner strength to rise to a challenge despite their own fears. You have shown all that just in this one day." Professor Abner sighed and stood up, straightening his jacket. "I know it's difficult to understand right now."

Ashley Kaplan

I shook my head. "How can I possibly live up to your expectations?"

"You've already surpassed my expectations, Arianna," he said. "But as for your skills, we will start work on those tomorrow. I suggest you get some sleep in the meantime."

He stood there for a moment, looking at me as if he might pat me on the head or something. Then awkwardly he said, "Right, goodnight then" and walked out of the training room, leaving me utterly alone.

I thought about going back to my room but my body was buzzing with energy. Now that I could feel this power, it wouldn't let me be. Instead of my room, my feet carried me to the courtyard. The compound slept and I was alone. Stopping into the center of the courtyard, I looked around. Spreading my legs apart in a defensive stance, I looked at my hands, wondering how I has used my power against the Infernal. I hadn't been thinking about it, it had just happened. Maybe if I could concentrate my efforts I could create something. I was an air sign, so the air was mine to wield. My eyes strained in concentration as I held my hands, palms up, before me. I felt the faintest wisps of air against my skin and then I saw it – a force of air gathering into a tiny circle, like a ball of yarn, between my open palms. My eyes widened in astonishment and my breath caught. Somehow I was channeling my power into a ball of energy. It looked like a swirling tornado inside a crystal ball. I raised it to eye level, trying to get a closer look, but I lost control of it and the ball flew full force out of my hands and straight ahead.

Damien stood at the other end of the courtyard, He had his hands held up to protect his face from the coming blow but it was as though the orb listened to him. Instead of deflecting it, he caught It. We both watched in fascination as he turned his hands around to cradle the orb but then it suddenly burst.

"I take it you couldn't sleep either?" I asked him.

"You trying to kill someone?"

I almost laughed. "We're in a fortress full of superheroes, not likely."

"What are you doing out here anyway?"

"I—none of your business. What about you?"

He folded his arms across his chest. "Ditto."

"Great, glad we cleared that up."

We stood at a stalemate, sizing each other up. Damien took a few steps forward, closing the distance between us.

"How did you do that anyway?" he asked.

I shrugged and lifted my palms. "I'm not sure. Just concentrated, I guess?"

"Can you do it again?" he asked, the challenge in his eyes.

There was no harm in trying. I tried to tune him out and concentrate on the air in the palm of my hand, hoping I could manifest it into something more tangible. It seemed to be working as a small ball formed in my palms but wisps were escaping; the ball was unravelling. Then I felt the warmth of Damien's hands, cupping my own, I don't know what possessed him to do that but it was electric. The touch of his skin sent shockwaves through me and I could see the ball getting stronger as the pressure built up. Then, briefly, Damien's thumb moved ever so slightly and as it glided across my skin I lost my concentration, the ball burst into nothingness.

I dared to look up at him; his gaze was intense as he looked into my eyes like he was trying to read something there. But then, without a word, his hands dropped to his sides and he raised an eyebrow.

"So what now? You going to join the army? Serve and protect and all that good stuff?" he asked.

"Yeah, right. I'm not so sure I'm cut out for it."

"Can't say I'm surprised."

"What's that supposed to mean?" I asked defensively.

"Look at you," he chuckled, "you're tiny for one. And… well…"

"Well, what?"

"There's nothing intimidating about you."

"You know, I assume being a jerk is an art form for you but in case saving your life didn't clue you in, I'm not your enemy."

Damien looked like he had just realized he was being rude and he sighed, running his hand through his hair. I noticed that it fell back over his eyes effortlessly.

"Yeah, I'm being an ass. I'm sorry. Look, it's just ever since I woke up in that alley it's been one thing after another and no clue about anything else."

"Dr. Levine said your memory will come back, you just have to be—"

"So help me if you say patient, I will break something." Damien shook his head. "It's just… why can't I remember?" He looked pained by what he couldn't reach in the recess of his mind. "WHAT can't I remember?"

"I'm sorry," I said gently. "It can't be easy, the not knowing."

"This is driving me crazy." He glanced at me. "You seem to be dealing well."

I chuckled. "If by 'well' you mean totally freaked out then yeah, I'm peachy." I sighed and sat down on a bench, running my hands down my thighs, agitated. "You may not remember anything, but everything I remember is a lie. I've got nothing to go back to."

He shrugged. "Well I guess neither of us had a real past before this."

"You know, Professor Abner was... I trusted him... now it turns out I was just a job to him."

"Guardians..." Damien mused. "At least you didn't get yours killed."

"Hmm, that's a plus."

"And you have your memory."

"Well, sure. Although those things are still trying to kill us."

"And we might be stuck here," he mused.

"But at least we have super powers," I said wistfully.

"Yeah..."

We let the words fall away into silence and allowed the full gravity of the day's events to sink in. It was like walking through a dream. Damien was angry; he made no effort to hide it and I supposed if I was in his place I would be too. But I wasn't in his place. I was still reeling from the lies I'd been fed my entire life. People I trusted, families that took me in.

They knew. Abner made sure they knew that I was special. That I was to be treated differently. One would suppose the thought would give me comfort but I couldn't help feeling cheated. Damien was right about one thing – neither of us had a past before this. My real life was well and truly only beginning today.

Drops hit the water, one after another, slowly and steadily. The sound echoed all around me as I opened my eyes. Everything was dark and murky, my body laying flat against a smooth, cold surface like stone. As I pushed against it to get up, I ran my hand across the surface. No, not like stone, I thought, it was stone.

I tried to focus my vision but it was no use. I couldn't seem to see anything clearly. Only blurred lines, ever moving like a flowing river. I stood and felt a few steps ahead of me. How much ground was there? I couldn't be sure yet this place seemed somehow familiar.

"You have returned, Solum," a female voice said from the shadows. Something struck me when I heard her; a memory somewhere beyond the deep.

"Who's there?" I called out.

"I sense fear in your voice. Why then did you return?"

"I don't know. Have I been here before?" I felt so confused, trying to reach into my memories.

"You have to return it. It belongs to me."

Then something clicked. I'd had this conversation before. Just yesterday I'd had this same dream. I was dreaming! But just like last time, something about this felt eerily corporeal.

"Yesterday... you said the same thing," and knowing that I was dreaming gave me a sense of stability and courage. Maybe I could stand my ground. "Who are you?"

"I am what you are made of."

Now, this was starting to piss me off. "Can you stop with the whole cryptic thing already? I would love to just get a straight answer."

"You have my gift, Solum, can't you feel it? Just as your ancestors did when I graced them with my power."

"Your gift? Your power... you're a Zodiac!"

A clap sounded through the darkness, like water hitting stone.

"Indeed. I am who your people call Aquarius."

I had to put my hand to my stomach to calm my sudden nausea. This was way too much too soon. I'd only just found out these guys were real and now I was talking to one. How was this possible?

"What do you want from me?" I asked.

"You are the only one of your kind. You have to return it."

"That doesn't clear anything up," I said under my breath, rolling my eyes. "There is a whole city of Gifted you could go to."

"No," she said authoritatively, the word echoing around me. "Not like you, Solum. You may walk among them but this path you must take alone."

"Okay, let's try a different tactic. Where can I find it?"

"I do not know this," and as she said that, I thought I could hear a sense of sadness in her voice. "It was lost in the great fall. Seek the Baru, he will guide the way."

"Something of yours was lost and you want me to find it... great. That's just great."

"It is beyond my reach now but not yours."

The air around me began to grow cold and I shivered, hugging myself for warmth. Her sadness was seeping into everything around me, from the ground to the breath in my lungs. I began to feel the sting of pain inside me, losing my breath. My hand flew to my throat as I

Ashley Kaplan

opened my mouth to try to speak, to calm her down. No sound came out and I began to feel faint until my body collapsed onto the ground. My head hurt as it hit the stone, I could see a dimming blue glow coming towards me from within the darkness. If I just focused my vision, I would be able to make her out, I thought, just as my eyes closed and I succumbed to sleep.

*

I woke with a start in a panic, sucking in a deep breath, getting as much air into my lungs as my body would permit. I realized that I had been sweating, despite the cold I'd felt in my dream.

Was it a dream?

But even as I thought it, I knew there was something more tangible to it than that. Aquarius was real and she was speaking to me for some reason. Although I still burned from Professor Abner's deception, he was the only one with any answers for me right now. Hurriedly, I dressed in yesterday's clothes and set out to find Abner.

After getting lost a couple of times and getting redirected, I finally found my way to the cafeteria. The hall was massive with its concave ceiling and windows lining the walls. Long tables were at its center with benches on either side. Dozens of kids around my age sat laughing together, talking, and having breakfast. Seeing so many of them in one room had me feeling a little overwhelmed but the smell of coffee was enough to urge me forward.

I walked up to the buffet line and was served with a smile and a "good morning." After getting a muffin, some oatmeal, and a cup of coffee, I made my way to the tables. Suddenly I was in high school again, not knowing who to sit with.

"Hey, newbie," said a friendly voice. I turned to see Calypso, holding an apple.

"Oh, good morning," I said.

She smiled and nudged me with her elbow. "Come sit down. How was your first night?"

"Uh, it was interesting."

She laughed as we took a seat at a table with three other kids.

"This is Jonah, Alex, and Tracy. Guys, this is Ari."

I remembered Jonah as the guy who had winked at me yesterday when we got to the compound. He had an infectious grin and seemed like the kind of guy who was always in a good mood. I had to wonder how old he was. Jonah seemed younger than the rest of us. Alex and Tracy were new to me. Alex was sitting on the edge of the table, instead of the bench. He had a mess of short, red hair and green eyes that had an unmistakable twinkle to them. He was smirking at me, a thumb resting on his lower lip.

"New toy," he said in a low, smooth, voice. "I like this one."

Tracy seemed more serious from the way she sat and carried herself. Her bright red hair was in a tight bun, her green t-shirt tucked into khaki pants and combat boots.

"Stuff a cork in it, Alex," she said. "Don't mind him, he's a pig. Hey," reaching a hand to shake mine, "welcome to Astro."

"You survived the first day!" Jonah said, grinning.

"Half a day," Alex added in a lazy drawl with a mischievous smirk.

"Don't be such an ass, Alex," Tracy admonished. "How are you settling in, Ari?"

I sat down and cradled my coffee like the elixir of life. "Ok, I guess."

"It will get easier," Calypso said, then added, "Alex and Tracy here have the Gift of Aries."

"Both of you?"

"She's my sister, but other than that we have nothing in common," Alex said smoothly.

"Thank the Zodiacs," Tracy agreed with an eye roll. "Although technically I'm not a Giftie, like you guys. I'm only a legacy, I have no powers."

Alex gave his sister a meaningful look. "For now."

Calypso grinned. "Jonah here is a Virgo, and over eager. He just got his powers a few months ago."

Jonah seemed to be bouncing on his heels from youthful exuberance.

"Check this out," he said and held his balled fist out to me. I looked at it as he concentrated and his hand slowly opened. There on his palm seemed to be freckles, but they were glowing. If I looked closer, I could see that they mirrored the constellation of the Virgo Zodiac. Then after a blink, they were just plain old freckles again.

"What was that?" I breathed out.

"The mark of my Gift," he said excitedly, "pretty cool, right? what's yours?"

Calypso rolled her eyes. "Give her some time to ease in, kid. She just got here."

Tracy cleared her throat. "Would love to stay and chat some more but we have to cover maintenance on the servers today," she said to Alex. "It's nice to meet you, Ari, we'll get better acquainted I'm sure."

"See you later newbie," Alex hopped off the table and pointed a finger at me like he was shooting a gun, with a wink, then followed Tracy.

I watched them go and took a long, satisfying sip of coffee. "Finish up," Calypso intruded on my blissful moment. "Abner is expecting us."

*

When we arrived at the war room, Damien was already there, speaking with Abner over something that appeared serious. The professor seemed to be explaining something calmly and patiently, in the way I'd seen him do countless times in his classroom.

"Morning Abner," Calypso said as she strutted in. "Newbie," she nodded, acknowledging Damien. I followed behind with Jonah at my side. I was too agitated to sit so I opted to stand.

"Good morning Caly, Jonah. Hello Arianna, how was your first night?"

"Restless," I replied.

"Ah, yes, that's to be expected I suppose. Um, well, I gathered you here this morning for a briefing. First things first, we will need to get something more permanent set up for you and Damien now that you'll be staying with us."

"How long?" Damien asked.

"I beg your pardon?" Abner asked.

"How long do we have to stay here?"

Abner, Calypso, and Jonah all looked like they'd swallowed something awful. The answer hung in the air, unspoken. Nobody wanted to deal the news; they must have assumed it was obvious.

"You're not going to let us go home, are you?" I asked.

"Yes, well," Abner cleared his throat, "now that your powers have awoken you'll no longer be safe living outside the city."

"So we're stuck here," Damien raised an eyebrow.

"This isn't right, Abner. We have lives, people that are going to miss us."

Calypso looked at me sympathetically. "I know it's hard for you to understand, but now that the Infernals know where you are, they will never stop coming. They will never stop hunting you. Your blood is a beacon to those creatures. And if you want to stay safe and more importantly keep your friends and family safe, you will stay away from them. You will only put them in danger if you go back."

"What about our things? Clothes?" I asked.

Calypso smiled reassuringly. "We'll escort you back to get your things. Don't worry Ari, we'll protect you."

"Very good, Calypso. Thank you." Abner continued, "Now onto more pressing matters: Damien's brother may still be out there somewhere. We have to move on the assumption that he's still alive until we know otherwise."

"Now we're talking," Damien chimed in.

"How do we find him?" I asked.

"Our best bet is to seek out the Baru, he will be able to divine what we cannot see."

I felt my body tense up hearing those words. Did Aquarius know that this was going to happen? But if she could know that, how could she not know where she lost whatever it was?

"You will have to go immediately. There is no time to waste, I'm afraid."

Jonah stood up and clapped his hands and rubbed them in anticipation. "Alright, I better get the truck fuelled up for you guys and ready to go."

Before I followed the team out, I took one last look back at Professor Abner. Yesterday I would have been able to go to him with any question. Today I found myself wondering if he was the person that I should be going to. I decided to keep my dream to myself for now. At least until after I met this Baru.

But there was one thing…

"Professor Abner?" I asked, hanging back.

"Yes, Ari?"

"I was looking through some of the books, you know just getting to know the place. But I came across a word I didn't know."

"Oh?"

"Yeah, it was…um…solum?"

Abner looked introspective for a moment as he thought it over.

"That's an odd one," he said, "well I believe it is the Latin word for 'alone' if I'm not mistaken. Which book did you say this was in?"

"Nothing, no, never mind. Ok, thanks."

I rushed out of there before he could take apart my lie.

Aquarius had called me solum, *why would she say that I was alone?* Wasn't I surrounded by people who were just like me? I wondered briefly if I would see her again in a vision, maybe then I could ask her what she meant by that. Just right now though I tried not to think about that as we walked through the silver metal doors to the underground garage.

Damien and I gaped at the expansive, brightly lit room we found ourselves in. The garage was massive, allowing for around forty vehicles, near as I could tell. From trucks, to racing cars, and there was even a small tank taking up a spot in the corner. Damien had his eye on one thing only, a row of motorcycles parked along the left wall.

"Now we're talking," he said, stopping before the bikes and whistling with admiration.

"I take it you like bikes?" came a male voice to our right.

"Hey, you made it!" Calypso smiled cheerfully as she crossed him. "Guys this is Orion."

Orion had spiked dark hair and a wide grin. Wearing a leather jacket and aviator glasses, he looked like a pilot.

"These guys haven't even seen a road yet," Orion said about the bikes.

"Seriously?" Damien asked. "When can they go out for a ride?"

"I bet tomorrow is a good day to shred the roads."

"How fast we talkin'?"

"Hey, fan boys," Calypso called over. "Hop to it, we gotta go."

"Say goodbye to the fun toys," I said with a grin.

This time when we left the city limits, we watched as Astro city disappeared behind us and it made me nervous. I felt safe there, a luxury I no longer had anywhere else, but there were things I left behind. The only memories I had left of my parents. I had to get them back if I was going to be gone indefinitely.

"So this Baru," I started, "who exactly is he?"

"It's what we call the astrological priests," Orion explained. "They can use the celestial omens of the stars to divine the future. Among other things. He should have some answers for us."

"The current Baru has been in hiding," Calypso said. "Orion has the Gift of Sagittarius, for hunting and tracking. The Baru are very elusive but hunters like Orion have been keeping track of their movements."

"Current one?" I asked.

"The Baru is the keeper of the sacred books we call the Tetrabiblos," Calypso answered. "A series of three books that contain forbidden spells, hidden magics, and the translation to reading the omens provided by the stars. Only one Baru can exist at a time, to protect the secrets hidden within the texts."

"So what happens when the Baru dies?"

"The next one in line is appointed as the keeper of the books. He alone can use the texts to translate the omens."

"Great," Damien mumbled. "Well, I think we're due for some answers so let's get to finding the guy."

After that, it wasn't much longer until we found ourselves parking the truck below my apartment building. I took a deep breath and stepped out of the truck, Calypso and Damien behind me.

"Orion will keep the truck running, I'll stand guard down here while you two go up and pack your things."

I nodded and Damien followed me up to my apartment. I braced myself to say goodbye to my first real home. I was finally eighteen and old enough not to need a foster family, this was supposed to have been a permanent address for me. Had this been my life only yesterday?

"Make yourself at home," I told Damien as I headed to my bedroom and proceeded to dig in the back of my closet for a suitcase.

The one useful thing about moving around so much is that I didn't have much to pack. There were some photos of my parents that I kept with me throughout though. Throwing my clothes in heaps into the suitcase, I added a few personal belongings and some sentimental trinkets. I was just finishing up when I heard the door open and then a loud thud, followed by a scuffle. My heart leapt into my throat and I panicked, thinking the Infernals had found us.

Skidding into the main room of the apartment, I was ready for a fight, but instead saw Damien with his arm against Joel's neck, pinning him to the wall. Joel was squirming, trying to get Damien off of him, but he was unmatched when it came to brute strength. I realized, dumbly, that I was still staring at them and jumped into action.

"Get off of him!" I shouted, grabbing Damien by the arm, but he didn't budge.

"Not until he tells us who the hell he is. The guy just walked in!"

"Because we left the door open, you jackass," I snapped, my voice steadily getting higher. "Now get off him, Damien. He's a friend."

Damien reluctantly let him go and stepped back as Joel sputtered, gasping for air and rubbing his neck.

"Oh gods, Joel, are you alright?"

"Is he a lunatic?!" he demanded.

"Just overprotective… and a little aggressive, so in a word, yes."

Damien gave me a glare, saying he didn't appreciate the comparison.

"Ari, what the hell is this?" Joel looked warily at Damien and took me by the arm, pulling me away. "Where have you been?"

"It's kind of a long story and I really can't get into it right now. I'm sorry I worried you guys, I lost my phone—"

Ashley Kaplan

"You mean this one?" Joel interrupted as he pulled my phone out of his pocket. "Katie and I went looking for you when we realized you weren't picking up your calls. We found it in the alley at the university. We checked your place all day yesterday. You just disappeared."

I took my phone back and pocketed it, but I must have looked appropriately guilty because the next thing I knew Joel was wrapping me in a big bear hug. "I'm just glad to see you're okay. We should call Katie—"

"NO!" I pushed him away. "No, wait, don't call her, or she'll be on her way over here."

"So? what's the big deal?"

"Hey, buddy. She said no, deal with it," Damien added unhelpfully.

"I'm sorry, who the hell is Mr. Friendly again?"

"Look," I said gently, "everything is okay. I'm just going on a trip and I don't have time to explain it all."

Looking over my shoulder into my open bedroom, Joel finally noticed the suitcase on the floor and looked at me with narrowed eyes.

"Okay, Ari. You realize how this sounds right? Is it this guy? Is he taking you somewhere against your will?"

Damien rolled his eyes and chuckled at what I assumed he thought was an absurd question.

"I really can't explain it. You're just going to have to trust me."

"Trust you?" he asked. "Okay... so then when will you be back?"

I groaned inwardly. "I don't know."

"You don't—" he started, visibly flustered. "Is this some kind of joke?"

"I'm sorry I can't explain it any better. Right now, I need you to go. Tell Katie I'm alright, I will get in touch with you guys when I'm settled."

Even as the word came out of my mouth, a part of me knew it was a lie. This felt too much like a goodbye, but I wasn't ready to face that yet, if ever. I couldn't accept that this might be the last time I saw my best friend.

"Look, Ari, I don't know what's going on here but I will hold you to that. We'll be expecting a call."

"I promise," I said giving Joel a hug, hoping it wasn't the last one. When we pulled apart, he gave Damien a pensive look and then gave my arm an encouraging squeeze before he left. I found myself letting out a breath I didn't know I'd been holding, I hated lying to him like that, and at that moment felt incredibly defeated by my new situation. Pulling my suitcase out of the bedroom, I sighed.

"Okay, let's get out of here before any other surprises show up."

"That's it?" Damien asked, pointing at my one suitcase.

"Foster kid. I'm kind of used to packing light and quick."

"Sorry, I didn't realize," he said uncomfortably.

"No worries, I know it's not much," I gestured to the apartment, "but it's my first real home, you know? I thought I would stick around long enough to make some memories."

Damien tapped his head with a finger. "Memories are overrated if you ask me."

I realized he was making a bad joke at his own expense and I couldn't help but wince, though I was grateful for his attempt.

He grabbed a box full of my things while I pulled the suitcase along and locked my door, wondering if I was doing so for the last time.

Next, we headed to Damien's home. Abner told us that Damien and his brother Theron lived above a garage they both owned and operated with their Guardian, Owen Phillips. We pulled open the garage doors and parked the truck inside the shop. Car parts and tools were hanging off the walls and strewn atop counters. Oil-stained rags lay in a heap and there was one car with its hood up like it had been worked on recently. Damien surveyed every inch of the place and by the look on his face, he was trying hard to will the memories to mind.

It didn't appear to be working but as he walked behind the car and through a plastic curtain, we followed him to the back of the shop. In that smaller room, under flickering light, was a sleek black motorcycle. The silver from the metal shone under the light as though someone had just polished it recently. The leather seat looked brand new and there was not a scratch on it.

Damien crouched down to take a closer look and ran his hand across the smooth surface of the bike.

"A thing of beauty," he said appreciatively.

"Is this yours?" I asked.

"I rebuilt it from spare parts. Took me forever but she was worth it. I can't believe I remember."

"You took care of it well."

He stood up and patted the thing. "I won't be leaving this baby behind again. This beauty is coming with me."

I just looked at him in amusement.

"Hey, don't hate on the bike," he warned and his countenance was so serious I had to hold back my laughter.

We followed him upstairs to the apartment where the three guys had lived. It was pretty neat compared to the clutter of the garage below. The place was warm with a homey feel to it like a family had lived here. There were photographs on the wall of the three of them together, some had the brothers alone and I was amazed at how identical Damien and his brother were. There would be no way to tell the two apart by looks alone, I realized.

In one photo an older guy stood with a beer in hand, a flannel shirt on, and a baseball cap, with Damien on one side and Theron on the other, both boys with a beer cheering to the camera. I figured the guy in the center had to be Owen, their Guardian. Now he was dead, Theron was missing, and Damien had no memory of that life with either of them.

Seeing the pictures on the wall made me feel for Damien. He was losing so much. *Had* lost so much. I pulled the photographs off the thumbtacks and placed them in a box of Damien's things while he wasn't looking. He should have them, I thought.

"Alright, I'm all set, except for my bike."

Calypso looked confused. "How are we supposed to bring that thing back with us?"

"You're not. I'm going to ride it and follow behind."

"Damien..." she began but his face said it all. He wasn't going to leave his bike behind.

"Alright, but you better stay tight on our trail."

Damien offered her a wide grin. "That's not gonna be a problem."

*

The wastelands became dotted with spots of greenery the further we drove. The yellow sand turned a darker red. Soon the emptiness on either side of us was filled with greenery. Patches of grass, trees, and bushes dotted the roadside as we headed closer to the water. Ahead was the Great Lake, although only in name now since the water had dipped so low over the last hundred years. I realized that we were driving along the bluffs, atop the rocky walls above the water. I could see us nearing the peak where the cliff met the sky and a little house stood on its edge. It wasn't exactly hidden the way I had expected but it was certainly remote with no other habitation for miles. We parked the truck just beyond the trees, Damien right behind us on his bike, and the four of us made our way up the path towards the Baru's little brick house.

Orion and Calypso seemed to hesitate and both raised their hands, prepared to use their powers if need be.

"What's going on?" I asked.

"Something is wrong," Calypso answered.

Orion sniffed the air. "It smells like a wet dog. Can't you smell it?"

I shrugged. "I mean, I didn't want to say anything..."

"It's an Internal, they always stink," Orion said, lowering his voice.

I heard Damien crack his knuckles and watched his face change. He was ready to take his revenge on one of those things. I had faced two of them just yesterday and wasn't eager to go head to head with one again, but what did that mean for the Baru?

"He could be in there, hurt," I said.

"Or dead," Orion countered.

"We should leave them back at the truck. It isn't safe," Calypso said to Orion.

"Like hell," Damien protested.

"This isn't the time to throw your weight around," said Calypso. "You'll get your chance but today isn't the day,"

"We're wasting time," I said impatiently. Before I knew it, I had pushed past them and my feet were racing up the slope to the little house.

"Hey!" Orion yelled after me.

I wasn't sure what possessed me to run into danger but this guy had answers for me and I had been in the dark too long. I needed to find out what he knew about me. Sliding to a halt at the front door, I noticed it was ajar and pushed it open before taking a step in. The others caught up to me as I squared my shoulders, ready for battle. As we entered the house, Orion motioned with his finger for me to be quiet and gestured for Calypso to go right while he went left. She nodded, daggers in hand, and went to search the house. I could see that it was a mess, ransacked. Damien and I walked into the living room where furniture had been thrown about and a broken lamp lay on the floor, but there was no sign of the Baru. We barely heard the footsteps of the others as they walked through the house, which didn't take long as it was so small.

"The house is empty," Calypso said, relaxing.

"We're too late," Damien nodded towards the mess on the floor.

"Let's get out of here," said Orion. "We will regroup and figure it out later."

My disappointment was palpable but there was nothing else to do here. "This can't be it. There's gotta be some clue about what happened to him."

Damien raised an eyebrow. "Yeah. This is a real head scratcher."

I ignored him and walked past the furniture towards the center of the living room. Ever since I'd met him, Professor Abner had encouraged me to trust my instincts. I had to trust them now; there was something we were missing here. I took a step closer to the fireplace and paused. There was something odd about the way the ashes were spread over the bottom, like something had been rubbed in it or thrown around. Bending on one knee, I knelt to take a closer look. I thought I could hear a dull scratching sound.

"What is it?" Damien asked.

"Do you hear that?"

Before he could answer me, soot came flying out at us and blew over the room in a cloud. I covered my face, coughing, when I suddenly felt the air knocked out of my lungs as I was tackled to the ground.

"What the hell?" Damien shouted.

"I can't see!" Calypso yelled back.

Whatever was on top of me was hidden by the cloud of ashes. I could hear the rest of the group coughing but I was pinned down with what felt like sharp knives. My skin broke and blood began to drip from my arms and legs where I was being held.

"Get the hell off me!" I shouted.

As the ashes settled, the creature before me began to take form. The face was human but it had black claws which were now pinning me to the ground. He had the torso of a man but the rest of his body was a glistening black scorpion. The daggers I was feeling were his legs that were digging into me. His tail was raised over his shoulder, the stinger pointing at my head.

I could hear the rest of the gang stumbling around as they regained their vision. The terror creeping into me was quickly giving way to pain, so I latched onto that as hard as I could.

Just concentrate on the pain, I thought. *If you don't, he's going to kill you.*

Though my arms were pinned down my hands were free. I reached down as far as I could and grabbed hold of each of his scorpion legs. They were too thick and strong for me to do anything. The thing pressed harder.

I could see the others starting to get their sight back and heard Orion first. "Damn it, Calypso, watch out!"

"What is that thing?" Damien shouted from somewhere.

The pressure was mounting. There was too much pain now as my blood began to trickle down my arms and legs. I raised my palms and willed all that pressure to build… build… stronger from within the very pit of my stomach until I finally set it free.

The scorpion man went flying into the wall but quickly scrambled onto his feet. Calypso raised her hand and, with a flick of her wrist, lit a thin line of fire between me and the thing. He hesitated for a moment, giving me a chance to get back on my feet. I watched in horror as he began to walk backward and with his arachnids legs climb the wall and make it onto the ceiling.

Calypso tried to throw her daggers but he deflected those expertly with his tail, and soon I was looking up at him above me. He was preparing to lunge. My eyes darted to the floor where two of the daggers lay, just on the other side of the fireplace. I knew he saw me looking and just as he lunged at me I willed all my strength and, with a sprint forward, jumped over the fireplace and rolled, slamming into the wall. The scorpion man grabbed the couch and tossed it effortlessly at Orion and Calypso to subdue them as he came at me.

"You're not touching her," I heard Damien say and suddenly he was standing between me and the creature, only a wooden table leg in his hands. Not exactly a winning weapon, I thought, but he stood ready to fight this unbelievable beast. The creature narrowed his eyes and snapped his tail forward but Damien used the table leg to defend against the blow. The point of his tail struck home and got stuck in the wood; Damien and the beast trapped in a tug of war.

With a growl of frustration, the creature swung his tail sharply and Damien, who was still holding onto the table leg, was swung across the room into a dresser. Ash still in my eyes and fire heating the room, I could make out Damien as he struggled to get up.

"Ari, get the hell out of here! RUN!" Orion shouted.

The creature came at me again, slipping on strewn papers but never losing his balance. I stumbled and ran towards the front door as he came bounding after me. With every step, I knew he was going to catch up to me.

Inches away.

Moments.

Any second now.

Just as I reached the front door handle, he grabbed my arm and twisted my body back to face him. The door was flung open and slammed me further into him but this time I was ready. As I knocked into his stone-like chest, I saw his eyes bug out. He tossed me aside like a rag doll and I slammed into the open door, hitting my forehead and slumping to the floor. I heard the shrieking behind me before it finally stopped and there was nothing but stunned silence.

My head was pounding from the blow but I was still alive. I had grabbed hold of the dagger just before I ran and it was still in my hand when the creature grabbed me. I knew that I felt it cut against flesh.

"Did I kill it?" I groaned in pain.

As soon as the words were out of my mouth, I heard the unmistakable cocking of a chamber and looked up to face the barrel of a shotgun. He was small and wiry, with a tawny brown complexion and no hair on his head. Standing with legs apart, crouching low, he stared at us. The man wore a brown tunic of some sort which ended in loose, low-hanging pant legs and sandals.

"You better have a very good reason for being on my property."

"You're the Baru, aren't you?" I asked.

"Who I am is the one asking the questions around here."

"But you are him," I said shakily getting to my feet. I couldn't help smiling. "Are you alright?"

He faltered for a moment but caught himself. "I ask you again, what are you doing here?"

Damien took a step closer to me. "We just came here for some answers, we're…" he paused. "Legacies."

"Prove it."

Calypso stepped around me. She fanned her fingers wide and the flames she had conjured moments ago extinguished. The Baru closed his eyes in relief and lowered the gun. He let go of a deep breath and pushed past us into his home.

"Thank the Zodiacs. I'm not sure if I could have used this thing," he said about the gun and set it down. Calypso threw it over her shoulder as we followed him in.

"My name is Argus. I am indeed the Baru."

Damien paused and looked me over. He took hold of my arm gently and turned it. "You look like crap," he said but he was smiling.

I smiled back and pointed at the black gooey puddle on the floor. "You should see the other guy."

"Speaking of the other guy," Damien said, "anyone wants to share what today's brand of creepy crawly was?"

The Baru sighed and took the glass of water Calypso offered him. "That was an Aqrab. Closely related to the Infernals."

"What was it doing here?"

Orion answered, "Must have been lying in wait for the Baru."

Argus nodded. "The Infernals were here and one of Amelias cursed humans was with them. They took the Tetrabiblos."

"Did they see you?" asked Orion.

Argus shook his head. "No, I hid in the trees until they left. I had just come in to see the damage when I heard your car pull up. I thought maybe they were coming back so I grabbed the gun and left out the back door."

"So you can see the future but you couldn't see this coming?" Damien asked sarcastically.

The Baru gave him an annoyed grunt. "That's not how it works. You Astral Warriors are all the same – shoot first ask questions later. That's why you need us, we actually use our heads."

"Burying your head in a book doesn't help save lives."

"And you have saved many lives then boy?"

"Ok look," I cut in, "we don't have time for this."

"Ari is right," Calypso agreed. "We've had more Legacies attacked in the last two weeks than there have been in the last two years. Now they show an interest in the Tetrabiblos? That can't be a coincidence."

The Baru shook his head solemnly. "I fear that you are right. I did manage to save one book; they would be hard pressed to get far without it."

"What is it?" I asked.

"*Enuma Anu Enlil*. It is the translation that allows me to read the celestial omina."

"The what?"

"Omens, girl, omens, so that I may foresee what is to come."

"What about the other two books?" Damien asked.

Argus sighed. "They were taken. Those books are filled with cursed magics, secrets passed down to humanity by the Zodiacs themselves. With that kind of power…"

"Right, Argus," said Orion. "It might be best if you came with us. It's not safe here anymore. You should be in Astro City where we can protect you."

I turned away from them and took a deep steadying breath, my nerves on edge. I stepped over to the window, needing some fresh air to gather my shaken confidence. Their voices faded in the background as I took a deep breath in but then a stirring in the trees caught my eye. A stark black shape against the deep green of the woods. A girl staring right at me, unwavering, through the trees. She looked like an apparition, beautiful and alone like she didn't belong there. With a blink and a shake of my head, she was gone, and I had to wonder if I had imagined her.

The Baru sighed in resignation and I turned back to him. "I have to agree with you, young man," he said to Orion. "I have been keeping an eye on the stars. Things are moving too quickly now. I'm afraid we've run out of time."

"For what?" I asked.

"War, my dear girl," he shook his head in defeat. "War is at our doorstep."

When we returned to the compound we took the Baru straight to the war room to meet with Professor Abner. He was sitting behind the desk poring over some paperwork when the five of us walked in. Abner got to his feet immediately.

"Argus!"

"Abner?" the Baru said in surprise. "Is that you?" he asked squinting his eyes as if to see better.

Abner chuckled. "It's me, in the flesh."

The Baru looked uneasy. "Or something like it."

I looked over at Abner, the question in my eyes, but he shook his head as if to say it wasn't important.

"Gods, Arianna what on earth happened to you?"

My clothes were blood-stained and ripped, I had a fresh bruise on my forehead, and the rest of me was covered in soot and ash.

I shrugged. "Just took down an Aqrab, no big deal." I faltered. "it's Aqrab right? I'm saying it right?"

"Took down? You mean you killed it?" There was real concern in his voice as he closed the gap between us. He was looking me over, assessing the damage.

"Your girl did good, Abner," Calypso said with a grin.

"I should say so…" he let the sentence trail off and looked at me in wonder. Again there was that spark of pride in his voice. No doubt he was patting himself on the back for the fabulous job he did training me without my realizing it. But then he snapped back to the present.

"You should visit with the doctor as soon as we're done here." He cleared his throat. "Please everyone, have a seat," Abner said and we all gathered around the round table.

The Baru held the last remaining book from the Tetrabiblos in his hands as though it would melt away. The cover was made of brown leather stretched tightly over the paper. The pages were well preserved although tanned by time and wear.

"Will you divine for us old friend?"

The Baru looked over Professor Abner critically but then he finally nodded and placed the book on the table before him. Opening it to the center, Argus placed both hands on the pages, lifting his head to the ceiling and closing his eyes. The words, which were inscribed in a language I couldn't understand, seemed to shift on the pages. They crawled slowly across the parchment up the Baru's fingers and over the backs of his hands then up to his forearms. They seemed to seep into his very veins. When Argus opened his eyes, a glowing silver light shone in his pupils. He was aligned with the universe, seeking answers from the stars and I was in awe.

"Ask your questions Davy Abner," the Baru spoke in a voice that sounded distant, apart from him.

Professor Abner cleared his throat. "Where can we find Theron, Bardin?" he asked.

There was a long pause as the Baru waited for the answer from the stars.

"I do not feel this energy," he said finally.

"Look again," Damien growled at him.

"The stars cannot see this life force."

By the looks on everyone's faces, I could tell what we were all thinking. Theron Bardin was likely dead. My heart ached for Damien at that moment. First Phillips and now his brother. There was nobody else to give him answers, no part of his past left. He clenched his jaw and turned away, then in a moment of frustration he grabbed hold of a chair and swung it against the wall. I flinched but nobody spoke; we all understood the pain he must be feeling.

Abner swallowed hard but pressed on. "The Infernals' attacks have gotten more frequent. More desperate. We need to know why."

The Baru was silent for a long time. I thought maybe his mind was gone, stuck in a trance until, finally, he answered.

"I cannot see her motives but there is something else…" His eyes remained blank but his features rounded in amazement. "How transcending…" he whispered in awe. "Miraculous."

"What is it?" Damien growled impatiently.

"The universe is re-aligning and the stars will shift ever so briefly. For the first time in six hundred years, this alignment will fall on the Observation of the Ascendant. With the right spell, such an event can open a crack in the door that keeps us from the heavens themselves."

Abner's face became ashen. "This spell, it wouldn't happen to be contained within the Tetrabiblos would it?"

"That and much more."

"That's what I was afraid of," Abner said quietly. "How long do we have?"

"One year and fifty-six days until we witness the glory of the gods."

"What exactly does this mean, Abner?" Orion asked.

"The Observation of the Ascendant is a day when people gathered to give thanks to the Zodiacs. The stars alignment allowed the doors to the heavens to open, receive the sacrifices. Once the Zodiacs disappeared, humans were shut out. But if the doors were forced open then Amelia won't have to come after us anymore."

Understanding was beginning to dawn on all of us then. "She will be able to go after the Zodiacs directly," I said.

"It makes sense now why the Infernals are on the move," Damien said. "Amelia knows the Astral Warriors won't just let her stroll right through the gates."

I nodded. "The more of our kind she neutralizes, the less of a fight she will have."

The Baru shook his head. "All paths lead to destruction."

Abner pushed away from the table, standing. "Thank you, Argus."

"There is something else…" the Baru said, a look of confusion on his face. "The stars are shouting at me." His brows knitted. "An anomaly?" He paused. "A cusp sign!"

Calypso shook her head. "Not possible, we would know."

"There's no way," Orion said.

"What's a cusp sign?" I asked.

The Baru lowered his head and then turned it towards me. His eyes seemed to shine brighter now that he stared into mine. I watched with bated breath as his face became pliant, clear, and understanding came to him as the stars provided the knowledge he sought.

"It is you," the Baru said evenly. "You are the anomaly. You are the Child on the Cusp"

Ashley Kaplan

All at once, the light flickered out of his eyes and the letters seemed to burn off his skin and turn to smoke. Now it was just Argus again, his link to the stars severed, and all eyes turned to me.

"Impossible…" Orion said in disbelief, but he took a step away from me.

Abner instead began to slowly inch closer as he looked at me with fascination. I felt like a museum exhibit that nobody could understand.

"What the hell is he talking about, Abner?" Damien asked.

"Peculiar…" Abner said quietly. "You see, when the Zodiacs gifted the mortals with their powers they had only one law, but it was absolute. The Gifted could only mate with non-powered mortals. The Zodiacs would not allow someone to exist who could wield the gifts of two gods. Because there was no telling how powerful such an individual would be, we were never meant to have those kind of abilities. It was forbidden."

Damien raised an eyebrow. "You saying this never happened before?"

Abner shrugged. "Well there were those who tried but the children were usually too supreme, their powers unpredictable even in the womb. The mother and her offspring never survived such a pregnancy."

"Until now," Calypso said while eyeing me warily.

"So what exactly is a cusp-whatever?" Damien asked.

Professor Abner seemed thoughtful before he answered. "Well, a Child on the Cusp is someone who is born in between two zodiac signs. Their powers are right on the cusp where one zodiac ends and another begins, meaning they can draw from both. Hence the name. Theoretically we can assume these children may possess powers that surpass either one of their counterparts, it would be the closest to godly power we could ever get."

I shook my head. "Abner this is ridiculous, obviously my mother survived my birth, Argus made a mistake."

"What kind do you think she is?" asked Orion, ignoring me.

"Not any kind," I said in irritation. "Are you listening to me? it's not true."

Abner stood before me, holding his hands out.

"It's alright, Arianna, we can sort this out. May I?"

I was afraid of the answers. Living in ignorance had been a safe place for me until now. I wasn't ready for so much change, least of all anything like this. Yet there was something inside me that couldn't help but wonder. Could this be real? My curiosity outweighed my fear as I placed my hands in Abners, palms up, then curled my fingers.

"Close your eyes," he instructed and I obeyed. "Take deep, steadying breaths. There is nothing and no one but you. Listen to the sound of your breathing, drown everything else out. Feel the gift of the Zodiac as it courses through your veins, fills your lungs, and breathes life into you."

I let my mind go quiet; I let everything else fall apart except Abner's words and the feeling of my power, the one I was just getting to know.

"Good," he said. "Now let it go, let the power come and manifest itself."

I uncurled my fingers and heard the gasp around me. Opening my eyes, I watched what looked like illuminated freckles on my palms. In the right hand, the freckles formed the constellation of the Pisces Zodiac. In my left hand, the freckles formed the constellation of the Aquarius Zodiac. My eyes widened in disbelief as I snatched my hands away, the visions instantly fizzling out as though they never were.

"So it is true," Abner said thoughtfully. Although his voice was calm, his face gave away his astonishment. "it would appear that you are indeed the Child on the Cusp."

"So my father…"

Abner nodded. "I'd wager he is one of the bloodlines we had lost track of. Likely, he didn't even know."

"An accident?" Calypso said in disbelief.

"An anomaly," Damien corrected.

I shook my head slowly, trying to deny it, trying to shake away the truth of what I was seeing. Argus stood and shut the book before coming to stand before me. "Do you realize what this means?" He was looking at me but speaking clearly to Abner. "This could be what turns the tide of this war. This girl could be the key to finally extinguishing the flame of the Cursed One."

"Now, old friend" Abner tried to reign in Argus' enthusiasm, "we know nothing of her powers, the fact that she even survived her birth is a miracle."

Argus shook his head fervently. "She is not just another Astral Warrior Abner. Can't you see? This girl is the weapon of the gods."

"NO," I shouted. "You have the wrong person, this… this isn't… it's a mistake."

"It is no mistake child." He started to reach toward me but I flinched back.

"I can't be here right now," I said pushing past them. "I have to go."

I ran aimlessly through the halls, trying to blow off some steam, my mind racing a million miles a minute. I didn't want this responsibility. I didn't want to fight a war, uproot my life, or say goodbye to my friends. I just wanted this to be over so I could go home and get back to my normal, uncomplicated life. I couldn't think straight, having more questions than ever before. Turning a sharp corner, I wasn't sure where I was going when I bumped straight into what felt like a brick wall. It would have knocked me backward but two strong arms reached out and grabbed me by the shoulders to steady me.

"Hey, woah!" It was Damien. "There you are. You ran out of there so fast, are you okay?"

I blinked. "Sorry, I wasn't watching where I was going."

He raised an eyebrow. "Where *are* you going?"

I shook my head, my eyes glued to the ground. "I don't know. I just can't be here right now. This is all too much."

He gave me a knowing half smile. "Yeah, I'm with you there. If you want to get out of here, I'm game."

I looked up at him, hopeful. "How?"

He thought for a moment before I saw a smirk cross his lips. I realized that Damien had kind of a nice smile. Too bad I hadn't seen him do it too often. "I've got an idea," he said, "Come with me."

Damien let go of my shoulders and grabbed me by the hand, leading me down the hallway. I wasn't sure if he realized he was still holding my hand as he walked but I didn't feel like pulling away. His palm was warm in contrast to the cold hallways of the training compound. The human contact gave me little comfort but I couldn't refuse it, I needed something comforting right now... familiar. With a sudden jerk, he pulled me back and pressed me up against the wall, pinning me with his body. His face was inches from mine and I could detect a musky scent.

"Um... Damien, what are you—"

"Not that. There are people coming around the corner," he said in a hushed voice that came out ruggedly sultry.

"Playing it a little cliche aren't we?" I whispered.

He actually smirked at me. "Oh what? Would you rather be the one pinning me to the wall? I always liked a woman in charge."

I could hear their footsteps as they got closer to us.

"If you keep looking like that, they'll think I'm attacking you, and then we'll definitely be stuck here."

Narrowing my eyes I reached my arms up and around his neck; his whole body felt so much warmer than mine. He was so close that I could feel his breath on my skin as I looked up into his eyes. It would only take a small movement to close the gap between us. I wondered briefly what he would taste like...

Damien stepped back from me so suddenly I nearly lost my footing, stumbling forward. "All clear, let's go."

Shaking my head, I let the disturbing images dissipate from my mind. Just like that, whatever moment I was obviously having with myself was gone.

I followed him until we ended up in the garage. The main lights were off but there were several bulbs still offering a dim glow. Damien stopped in front of the bikes.

"No," I said immediately.

"Don't be a coward now. It will be less noticeable than a car."

"And what if we run into any trouble?"

Damien dug into his pocket and pulled out the brand new cellphone that we'd each received from Abner before we'd left today. He waved it between his fingers. "Then we call for help."

I sighed and ran my hand through my hair, my need for distance outweighing my concerns. I nodded and got another smile from Damien. We walked the bikes out of the garage until we were at a safe distance and once we were sure nobody could hear us, we drove out of the city. The wind whipping at my bare arms was sobering, I needed that right now. I'd felt like I was on some sort of high ever since my powers awoke.

Damien and I stopped our bikes on a cliff overlooking Astro City. He rested his arms on his bike handles. Gone was the smile; there was only a troubled guy with a heavy weight to carry. The city was aglow with an opalescent greenish blue light. It felt alive somehow and I couldn't help but be amazed at what a well-kept secret it was. The golden dome that made up the training compound stood tall and proud in the center. It was so much less daunting looking at it from the outside like this.

I leaned against the bike with a heavy sigh, hugging my arms across my chest. Other than the city there was nothing for miles but dirt and sand. The sun had baked everything all day but by the evening there was a welcome chill in the air.

I could feel Damien looking at me but my eyes were glued to the view. The breeze felt cool against my warm skin, blowing strands of hair out of my face. I was mesmerized by the glowing lights of Astro City.

"So, how does it feel, knowing you're special?" he asked. The way he said it made me sound like I was different to him but I felt so much the opposite. Strangely I felt a closeness to Damien.

"You're special too," I said gently.

He chuckled, a self-mocking sound like he didn't believe it. His hair fell over his face as he gave me a boyish smile and raised his eyes to me.

"Not like you," he said warmly.

His words were like a caress and I was struck by how handsome he was when he smiled like that. The way he looked at me made my cheeks burn. I suddenly found myself feeling self-conscious but I didn't know how to respond to him. I'd been told that I could turn the tide of this war. The Baru had divined it from the stars themselves but I didn't see many scenarios where I made it through this. I barely had a grip on these powers and most of all I didn't want this responsibility. There was no scenario I could imagine in which this ended well for me.

"Yeah, well, I'm not so sure that's a good thing. I have a gnawing feeling that I know the ending to this story."

"Ari," he started, "it's not going to end like that."

"How can you be so sure?"

"Because I'm not gonna let it," he said. It was almost convincing. "Besides, if you want to take down Amelia, you'll have to get in line." I could hear the bitterness dripping from his every word. Gone was the gentle boy from moments ago.

"This isn't going to be one of those revenge at the cost of your life type of deals is it?"

He wouldn't meet my gaze. "If it comes to that."

"We don't know anything about her; we have no idea how to fight her, not to mention that neither of us are killers."

"That we know of."

"What?"

"I can't remember anything before two days ago, thanks to Amelia. For all I know I could be a killer."

"Damien…" I couldn't find the words to reassure him.

"And what about you? You took down that Aqrab easily enough today."

"You think that was easy?" my voice squeaked. "It took everything in me to summon just a tiny bit of force to push that thing off. Just look at my face, Damien, or the rest of me for that matter. I look like the 'after' picture on a survivor show."

Damien stared at me strangely but his face was stoic. "You haven't even realized have you?" He shook his head. "Ari, look at yourself. Your body has already started to heal, freakishly fast in fact."

"That's impossi—" but I couldn't finish the word. Looking over my arms, I pulled on the skin and saw that Damien was right. There was still bruising but the bulk of my injuries was disappearing, already scabbed over and looked like they were healing.

"How?" I whispered.

"Probably another side effect of all the Zodiac steroids in our blood. Face it Ari, you're not normal. I know *I'm* not normal but you're… extra."

"Are you making your way to a point?"

"All I'm saying is that whatever this cusp sign thing is, it makes you a threat. And that makes you—"

"A target?"

"I was gonna go with extraordinary."

Suddenly I was very grateful to the darkness for hiding my crimson cheeks from him. Nothing about Damien felt inviting, but his words felt honest to me, and that was better than any kind of gentleness he could offer. I found myself appreciating honesty more and more these days.

"That's flattering, but killing Amelia? you saw those things she controls. And we know she's not afraid to draw blood. She's got powers we aren't prepared for."

"She owes me my brother's life and my memory of him," he said simply.

That was one thing I understood without fail; Amelia's devastating actions had awoken our powers. We could have lived the rest of our lives oblivious to this world. Instead, we were gearing up for a war we were not prepared for. Thrown into roles that were foreign to us.

I looked back at Astro City with a renewed appreciation; there was so much going on behind those walls. So many innocent families in hiding because their children were called to the life of a Gifted. Then I wondered what would actually happen if the Gifted were all wiped out and there was nobody to stand in her way. With the Infernals at her command and the Tetrabiblos in her possession, there was no telling what Amelia could do. I wondered about Katie and Joel, oblivious to this world, and how Amelia's victory could affect their existence. That made me think of all the other kids, like me, who were out there with no idea that they were a walking target.

"There are probably more Legacies out there just like us being hunted down right now," I said.

Once I spoke the words aloud, I knew something had shifted inside me. I was scared and I didn't quite believe the whole cusp thing but I couldn't sit idly by while innocent people like Theron were disappearing. While Katie and Joel were out there in a world that could crumble. Maybe if we stopped Amelia, I had a hope of saving them, protecting their world from this one. If I could help end this war, there might be hope for the rest of us too.

"We have to stop her, don't we?" I asked, but I knew the answer.

"The best way to do that is to join the Astral Army," Damien echoed my thoughts.

I didn't respond, there was no need. As we both turned our heads back to the view before us, the unspoken words hung in the air and sealed out fate. We had just reluctantly accepted our new roles as Astral Warriors in the Zodiacs' army. I feared that if we didn't stop Amelia there would be no life for me to go back to anyway.

Ashley Kaplan

Pisces
Aries
Taurus
Gemini
Cancer
Leo
Virgo
Libra
Scorpio
Sagittarius
Capricorn
Aquarius

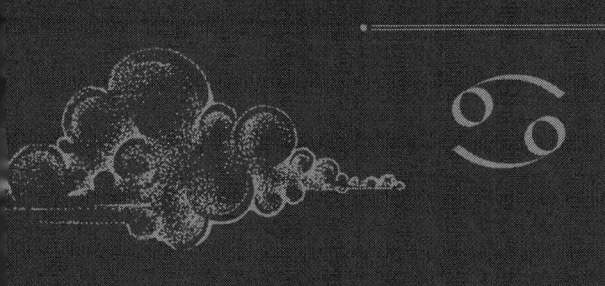

Amelia

A barren wasteland was the exhibit for her gallery. Amelia stood regal and tall on the high balcony, her graceful fingers curled over the railing. Hazel eyes with green flecks were scanning the horizon for something that she knew would never come. Her honey brown hair was caught in the breeze, framing a long face and high cheekbones. She made a beautiful masterpiece against the tableau of brown. The pale blue dress she wore accentuated her curves and ran down the length of her body, pooling at her feet.

She had once thought the throbbing pain in her heart would eventually turn into a dull ache but with each year she was proven wrong. Looking into the distance, Amelia could clearly recall the fertile land that once was and the fields of waist-length grass that grew there. She heard the echoes of laughter even through the deafening silence now, searching for the mop of hair where the sweet little boy was hiding. The centuries fostered her agony and inflamed her anger. She would not cry. Not ever again would she give those wretches the satisfaction, sitting atop their thrones in the sky, looking down at humanity in amusement.

"Mama what is that?" she heard the child's voice so clearly.

"That's a minnow, little one. See, there's more over there."

She watched the smile on her son's face brighten and the glimmer in his eye as he decided to catch it. Amelia stepped into the river, ankle deep, and watched as the boy threw his hands in the water and splashed all about, trying to catch the minnows. She couldn't help but laugh at the sight. His honey brown hair shone under the light of day and his skin was sun kissed just like hers. Amelia put her hand to her stomach; she was certain that there was another life growing in her belly, but it was too soon to show.

"That has to be the most beautiful sound I have ever heard," said a deep, light-hearted, voice behind her.

Amelia smiled brightly and lowered her eyes shyly. How was it that this man could still give her butterflies? Or perhaps it was the baby?

"Welcome back, my love. How was your outing?"

"Quite fruitful," the man said as he wrapped his arms around her waist and pulled her closer. "There will be enough for a pelt this winter for our little man."

"And what if we might need more than one?" she asked with a coy smile.

"What does he need more than one for?" he asked with a chuckle.

Amelia took hold of his hand and placed his open palm over her flat stomach. "It would not be for him."

Realization dawned as he looked down at her stomach and back up. "Are you certain?" he asked.

"I think so."

He raised his hand and cupped her cheek. Amelia leaned into it happily. "Woman, you truly are amazing."

His lips found hers in a kiss that held all the promise of the life they were building together.

Amelia knew she was lucky to have married the love of her life. Growing up in the same village, she'd seen the older boy as he played and studied but he paid no attention to her. As the years went by, she grew into a young woman, her limp hair gained volume, and her body began to fill out with curves. The boy she knew had turned into a young man, charismatic and always smiling, learning to hunt and work with his father. She had not the courage to approach him but she always watched when he was out in the square and smiled shyly to herself. If only she was braver she would speak to him, but what could she do?

The day everything changed for them was the day of the big storm. The diviners knew it was coming and everyone was preparing to greet the rain. People were penning up the animals and bringing loose items indoors to protect them from the wind. The entire village was buzzing with busy work and as the sky turned more gray the streets emptied.

"Oh no, Mama!" Amelia gasped. "We forgot to bring Odessa inside."

"Where is the old goat?"

"In the field, grazing. Mama, I have to get her."

"I don't like the looks of it out there, Amelia. I don't know."

"Don't worry, I'll run as fast as I can. At worst we will only get a little wet."

Before her mother could protest anymore, Amelia ran out the door and out to the field to get the goat. She found the little animal just where she expected and tying the rope to her collar, began the walk back home. But they weren't fast enough and the rain came down on them both. It only took minutes before they were soaked.

Amelia thought she could just run the rest of the way to the house but the wind picked up and began knocking her around. She used her arm to shield her face but she was having a hard time keeping balance and pulling Odessa along with her. Amelia cursed herself for her rotten luck as she slipped and should have fallen but then...

His arms were around her before she hit the ground. She tried to look up but the rain was beating down too strongly. She felt the grip on her and a tug on Odessa's rope as she was held firm and led into the village streets. Bursting through a door, they rushed into the building and Amelia heard it slam shut behind her. Her hair was wet and sticking to her face, her dress glued to her body. Chest heaving as she tried to catch her breath, she turned around to face her savior.

It was him, the boy she had watched, now the man that she had grown so fond of. He looked at her like she was a vision and Amelia could only imagine that she looked a mess. Here she was finally with an opportunity to say something to him but when her mouth opened all she could do was... laugh.

She began to laugh uncontrollably and after a moment of confusion, the young man joined her. They laughed so hard that they couldn't stand anymore and had to take a seat on the floor.

"The shop-keep will be very upset we let a goat in here," she finally said.

He shrugged and grinned. "Then we will have to be out of here before he returns."

"If this storm should ever pass."

"Do you have somewhere to be?"

"No," she smiled.

"Why have we never met before? This is a small village."

"I'm sure we have in passing."

"No," he said firmly, "I would have remembered you." That was said with a little more warmth and made Amelia blush.

"Well It's nice to meet you. I am Amelia," she said, reaching out her hand. He took it in his and heat spread throughout her whole body.

After that their fate was sealed and she had the rain storm and that goat to thank for it. Now here she stood with him as his wife, watching the life they had created for themselves.

Amelia closed her eyes and winced, willing the memory away. She needed it to stop. She didn't want to remember, but there was no use. Still, it came back to her like a sweet dream she could never grab hold of again. A beautiful nightmare.

Ashley Kaplan

She watched her husband and child together as the sun beat down and warmed her skin. Amelia could feel that warmth deep down into her very soul. There was little else she wanted out of the simple, wonderful, life she had.

*

Little did she know at the time that her happiness was measured in moments, and those moments were fleeting. Amelia closed her eyes, willing the painful memories to fade; she didn't want to let them in. If only she could hold onto the good ones and let the bad wash away with time. But it was no use. They broke through her wall, as they always did, and assaulted her mind with renewed ferocity.

Her precious boy, lying sick and pale on a cot. He was shivering as Amelia lay another blanket over him and kissed his forehead. Her loving husband looking just as bad beside him, coughed into his palm, the sound coming out like a bark. It had been nearly three weeks of this and they only seemed to get worse. The town healer could do nothing for them but manage their symptoms and after a while, even those medications weren't very helpful. She couldn't understand what was happening and why she was mostly unaffected. At first, she had experienced a small fever and some coughing, but her body fought it off, unlike theirs.

She feared that time was running out, so she decided to head out to the Temple of the Zodiacs and seek out help from them directly. Her husband wasn't as thrilled with her decision.

"They walk among the mortals," she said, "they gifted them with strength and health, surely they will listen to my plea."

"I don't like this, Amelia," he said with a shake of his head.

"All will be alright my love, you'll see."

She kissed her family goodbye and promised to return soon.

While the days were hot, the nights were frigid, but Amelia didn't care. She could barely feel the cold biting at her skin as she trudged one step after another to the temple. All she could do was pray to the Zodiacs, hoping they would hear her long before she arrived. As the sun broke, a farmer rode past her in his carriage and agreed to drive her the rest of the way, giving her legs some much-needed respite. Finally, two and a half days later, she stood before the alabaster building with its golden dome rooftop and wide set doors.

Carefully she removed her slippers and laid them by the door, took a deep breath, and walked in. The marble floor felt cold against her bare feet as she walked forward, her head hanging low in a humble gesture. There were several figures, they seemed larger than a normal person, dressed in finery. Some were lounging around, others were eating and drinking in merriment, and most were simply enjoying themselves. As Amelia reached the center of the room she dropped to her knees and bowed.

Ashley Kaplan

"Greetings, Zodiacs. I humbly come before you to beg for your help."

A woman stepped forward, kindness in her eyes and a sad smile on her face. "Welcome to our domain, we have heard your prayers all through the night."

Amelia raised her head, the tears behind her eyes threatening to burn their way out. For a moment there was a spark of hope in her. "I knew you would, I am so relieved. Please, I need your help, my child is sick and so is my husband, I no longer know what I can do for them."

The woman crouched down so she could look Amelia in the eyes and laid her hand on the back of her head in a comforting way. "My dear, I wish we could take their pain away, but what you ask for is a gift that we cannot give you."

"Cannot... but why?" she whispered, her voice cracking.

A man spoke beside her. "The gift of life is not simply just given."

Amelia swallowed hard and tamped down her hesitation, bravely speaking out. "I am prepared to give my life and the life of my unborn child, for theirs."

The woman sighed and stood back up, her smile fading to a frown. "We cannot tamper with death, sweet one. I know this is not what you were seeking but to give such a gift would have to be for an extraordinary purpose. This is not a life lost to unnatural means, nor is it valor or sacrifice. They are simply humans living out their destiny. We cannot interfere with that."

"No! You can't just turn me away!" she said in a panic now, her voice raised. "Why do you choose some but not others? How do you decide who is worthy of your gift? My family is innocent, they don't deserve this."

"I'm sorry, dear one, it is out of our hands. I am afraid it is too late for them."

Amelia felt like she had been slapped in the face and her pain turned to anger.

"NO!" she screamed out as she grabbed hold of a porcelain vase by the altar and smashed it against a wall. The entire room began to spin and she could no longer hear anything. Amelia felt as though her soul was sinking through the floor.

"We will send you home, dear one, so that you can save what precious time you have," she heard from somewhere in the distance.

Numbly, Amelia walked out of the temple, trying to force her tired muscles to run all the way home but when she blinked she was there. The Zodiacs had sent her home as they said. Her breath catching, Amelia felt like she was racing against time. Already she had been gone too many days. She floated in a haze through the house, searching for her husband and her son but there was nobody there. Her heart sank as fear took hold of her. She walked slowly through the back doors to the yard and there, under the shade of an oak tree, was fresh dirt in two piles as though it had just been dug.

Ashley Kaplan

The scream that tore its way from her throat sounded to her like it came from somewhere else as Amelia ran barefoot to the graves, dropping on top of the smaller one. The tears streamed so that she couldn't see the hands in front of her but she felt the dirt as she tried to dig down.

"No, please no, please. please," she cried hysterically. "I didn't say goodbye." She fell over, lying down on the smaller grave and curling into a ball, her hands caked in mud.

"My baby... my boy... come back to me. Come back... we were supposed to have more time." Amelia sobbed until exhaustion was too much to fight. The cold seeped past her skin and spread into her heart. She ran her hand over the dirt, imagining that she was stroking her boy's hair as she hummed to him like she always did before he went to sleep. Only now there was so much useless ground and dirt between them.

"Shhh, It's alright, I'm here," she said, her voice hoarse from crying. "I will stay with you, my darling." She sunk her cheek deeper into the dirt as she whispered, "with both of you. It's alright now. It's alright. It's alright.'

She didn't know how long she had been lying there but her body had finally stopped shivering. Maybe it was getting warmer or perhaps she had finally become as numb as her heart. All she wished for was to be buried in this grave with her family; she had nothing left to look forward to.

"There you are..." a voice spoke.

She opened her eyes at the sound, it was low and soothing, but Amelia wouldn't move.

"I could feel your anguish even from my corner of the earth."

She felt nothing, couldn't reply, nor did she care to.

"Such pain, so much heartache, I couldn't ignore it. Is this your family?"

She closed her eyes, willing the tears away, and nodded, her cheek scraping against the dirt.

"Ahhh" he breathed out slowly. "My dear girl. I don't normally interfere with the mortals in your part of the world." Amelia heard something heavy being dragged across the ground and the voice was suddenly right behind her. "But I cannot ignore your suffering, it echoes so very far, and I have come far to seek you out. Ask me what you will and I will try to help you. But know that my gift is a rare treasure. Do not take lightly what you ask."

Her eyes shot open. With him being so close now she could feel his breath on her skin. Amelia willed her aching muscles to pull herself up to a sitting position and lifted her head. Standing above her was the single biggest snake she had ever seen. His eyes were as dark as the night sky in a head that was twice her size. His body glimmered emerald green and ran the length of the yard, thicker than two tree trunks. She wanted to scream but her voice was too hoarse to allow much sound. Amelia squealed and scrambled across the ground, pressing her back against the oak tree, her heart racing and chest heaving in fear.

"Don't be afraid, my dear. I am not here to hurt you. Let me help you."

She shook her head. "What are you?" she managed to whisper.

"I am what you call a Zodiac," he said simply.

"That's impossible. I've seen the Zodiacs, they all have human forms, you... you are a snake!"

If he could smile, she thought that's what he was doing now. "Yes I am, but there are many of us. The Zodiacs you speak of rule here, in the Western world." As he spoke he curved his body and moved closer to her. Again, she heard the sound of the massive weight being dragged across the ground.

"My brothers and sisters rule in the far Eastern part of the world. While your gods ravage your lands together, my siblings sleep and only one of us is awake to rule at a time. This year is my time, the Year of the Snake. I watch over our mortals while my siblings slumber and rest. Next year my brother the Horse will wake and I will go back to rest until it is my time again."

Amelia swallowed hard and tried to calm her nerves. She recalled hearing some stories as a child about such things but never had she believed in any of them. Yet here stood proof, before her eyes, and how could she dismiss it? Especially when a Zodiac was offering her help.

"Can you bring them back?" she asked, her voice catching.

"I'm truly sorry, dear one, but I cannot tamper with the natural order of things. Not when their deaths were by natural means."

She narrowed her eyes at the rejection. "Then there is nothing you can do for me."

"Perhaps you need a day to reconsider. I do not make gestures like this lightly. In fact I have only ever helped one other from your realm. Her pain had called to me just like yours did. But giving Eve my gift did not end so well."

"Eve?" Amelia gasped. "You are the snake from Eden?"

He nodded his head. "Indeed, that was me. Your gods were furious. One, in particular, was very perturbed that I interfered. Can't recall which one it was, it is so long now. I had promised not to interfere again but... I cannot ignore your pain."

He turned his head and lowered his massive body to the ground, slithering away. He stopped only to look back and add, "I shall return tomorrow to offer one more time. There will not be another chance after that."

Amelia spent a fitful night sleeping on the cold, hard, ground by the graves. She couldn't believe that a Zodiac was offering something to her but she wanted for nothing other than her family. The longer she thought about it, the angrier she became. How dare those bastards sit on their thrones and judge who is worthy of saving? What made her family unworthy? What made her perfect, beautiful, happy little boy unworthy of saving? They had no business allowing some to have Gifts while others went without. Others who were in desperate need of help. Right then and there Amelia knew what she wanted. What she needed to do to feel some sort of peace in her dead heart. She needed to exact justice. She needed to exact revenge.

When the Snake returned the next day, Amelia met him in a praying pose, on her knees and bowed low to him.

"Thank you for returning."

"Have you decided? Do you seek knowledge, or strength, or perhaps immortality so you can start anew?"

"I would like a gift of your power, the fire that you possess within you to also burn within me."

The Snake shook his head slowly. "That is not a gift, it is a curse. Mortals under the Western Zodiacs domain can not carry the power of my siblings and me. This power is in conflict with what makes up your soul."

"I don't understand."

"Your soul is created from a different void than my people. This is the way your gods molded you. I can only gift such a thing to the mortals in my domain without risking peril."

"With deepest respect, Zodiac, my soul is already cold and broken inside. You asked what I wanted and it is your fire I seek. Perhaps it will warm my soul back to life. Without it, I may never find strength or warmth or... love," she said the last word bitterly, "again."

The Snake recoiled as if stung. "Your pain is so, deep dear one, even now its echoes assault me with their magnitude." He seemed to sigh and pulled his body into a tight circle.

"The child you carry will likely not survive your curse. Are you prepared to lose this one as well?"

Amelia's hand instinctively went to her stomach; she had forgotten all about this new life. But what about the life of her son?

"I have made my decision."

The Snake sighed, his tongue flitting in and out of his mouth. "As you wish."

Amelia snapped out of the memory at the sound of the knock on her balcony door.

"Mother?" a female voice called out.

She didn't bother turning around. "Yes?"

"It was right where we thought. We recovered the Tetrabiblos."

Ashley Kaplan

Amelia smirked to herself. She had found it, after years of searching. Years of Baru after Baru taken down along with their Guardians and their Gifted. Finally, she was one step closer to exacting her revenge. She turned to face her daughter with a bright smile.

"Thank you, Imani. I will be down shortly."

The girl nodded and gracefully exited, leaving Amelia alone. The woman watched her daughter go and mused over the strange twist of fate. How was she to know that the Snake's gift would strengthen the life within her? It was a miracle, the only solace she had from the nightmare that she survived. Together they would get justice for their family. Imani was a powerful girl, a Westerner touched in the womb by the power of the Eastern Zodiac. There was no other like her and Amelia had to admit she was proud. Far from the young girl that laughed at that river bank once upon a time, the Zodiacs' fire had kept her alive and kept fanning the flames of her ire. Their day was coming, the Western Zodiacs would soon be nothing more than the stories they were believed to be.

Aries
Taurus
Gemini
Cancer
Leo
Virgo
Libra
Scorpio
Sagittarius
Capricorn
Aquarius
Pisces

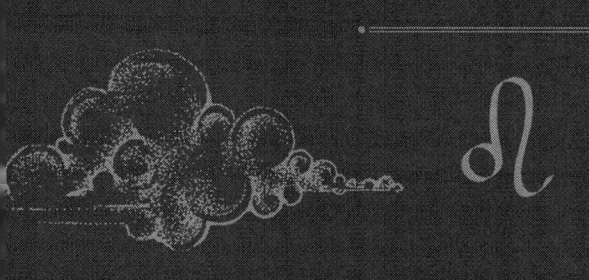

Becoming

Cold and hard stone touched my cheek as my eyes fluttered open. I felt the smoothness of the rock beneath my hands and looked around. The same darkness I was beginning to know so well surrounded me, the only visible light shone above me in one single ray, illuminating me. I looked up and wondered for the first time If I was underground. I heard the drop of water... drip, drip, drip. Perhaps this was a cave?

Using my hands to push myself up I looked around. "Are you here?" I asked, for once taking charge of the narrative.

"Hello?" I called and heard the echo around me.

"Keep your voice down, we're trying to sleep," she answered.

This time I wasn't afraid of her. "Aquarius," I breathed out her name; her familiarity was somehow soothing to me even amidst this foreign place. Or maybe it was that my power was responding to her presence.

"I'm sorry," I lowered my voice. "I didn't mean to disturb you. Why do you keep bringing me here?"

"I do not bring you, solum. You shouldn't be allowed in this place between worlds and yet... here you are."

"Between worlds?"

"It looks like your world and yet it is not. You appear to be in mine, yet you are not."

"How is that possible?" I tried to find her in the darkness but her voice seemed to be coming from all directions.

"Your gifts bring you closer to us," she said. "This insurrection of our law and your existence is tolerated for now, Solum, for you are the only one who stands a chance to restore it."

"What?"

Ashley Kaplan

"Death will resurrect where new life is given; a dip in the wrong hands will summon the vision."

"Please, I want to help you but I don't understand what you're asking."

"You must find it before she does. You must. Lest our enemies bathe in all our blood."

"You're afraid," I whispered stunned.

Before she could respond, I felt myself slipping away and I knew I was being pulled back. The light above me dimmed until it was gone completely and I was left in an abyss.

"Aquarius?"

*

"Hello? Earth to Ari!" Calypso came up behind me.

I snapped my head up and blinked at her, disoriented.

"Abner wants us in the council chambers," she said.

I hadn't spoken to her since yesterday and wasn't sure what she thought of my new status. I guess I was going to find out soon enough. I followed Calypso out of the cafeteria and down different halls, still having no clue how to maneuver through this grand place, wondering if I would be here long enough to learn.

"So, should I bother asking what this is about or is it kind of obvious?" I asked sarcastically.

To my surprise, she offered me a sympathetic smile. "Yeah, you kind of took us all by surprise. There are so few of us Legacies, you know? And even a smaller number of those whose gifts awoke. Having a cusp child in the ranks changes the game. It helps even the odds. Even if we are low in numbers."

I raised my eyebrows with wide eyes. "Yeah... twenty-something people doesn't make much of an army I guess. Maybe against like really tiny Infernals?"

Calypso laughed. "Or stupid ones."

I shrugged. "Well, the ones I've met weren't exactly college graduates. I mean sure, I technically met my first one *at* a college."

"But you know there are more than just twenty of us in the Zodiacs' Army."

"But I thought—"

"Ari..." she chuckled. "We might be capable of great things but we can't fight all the Infernals. There are too many of them. Anyone can join the cause if they choose to. But only the Gifted can be Astral Warriors. Many of our soldiers are regular people who simply know the truth of what is going on. They live in their cities, countries even, just waiting for orders."

"I had no idea," I said. "So, what's with the council chambers? Why aren't we meeting in the war room?"

She hesitated. "Well after what the Baru divined last night, Abner had no choice but to alert the council members of your existence. The available ones have gathered today to meet with you and decide the next steps."

I rolled my eyes. "Super."

"It won't be so bad." She smiled at me as we stopped in front of a set of double doors. "Deep breath, you ready?"

I nodded with a shrug. I had no desire to meet the Council of Twelve. Yet since my powers awoke I had hurtled farther and farther down the proverbial rabbit hole with no sign of slowing down.

Time to see what lies through the looking glass, I thought to myself.

The council chambers looked like a courtroom with wooden pews on either side of a thin aisle. The aisle ended at a raised podium with twelve seats in a semi-circle. Before each seat was an illustration of a different zodiac sign, lit in glowing neon. Four of the council members were currently present – a woman and three men, sitting in their rightful places and looking down at me. Orion stood in the center of the room beside Damien who gave me a nod in greeting. Professor Abner stood to their left with that same austere look on his face I'd seen so many times before.

"Council members," said Abner, "I'd like to introduce to you Arianna March."

I swallowed the lump in my throat as I waited for them to point at me, call me a fraud, and throw me out of the room.

"Ms. March, Mr. Bardin," the councilwoman spoke, addressing Damien and me. "I am Alicia Townsgate and these are my colleagues Robert Wright, Ian Quentin, and Martin Lewis. Now that we've dealt with introductions, shall we get down to the matter at hand?"

"Which is what exactly?" Damien said gruffly, his arms crossed over his chest. I had to smile at his complete disregard for authority.

"For one," said the woman with a disapproving tone, "there is the matter of the Cursed One. You have information, Abner?"

Professor Abner nodded and took a step forward. "Yes, the Baru we brought here yesterday divined the celestial omina. He believes she means to strike on the Observation of the Ascendant. She also holds in her possession two books of the Tetrabiblos."

Martin Lewis looked alarmed. "That is grave news indeed. We have been getting accounts of several concentrated attacks in recent weeks. Whatever her end game is it would appear she is reaching her deadline."

"Amelia," Quentin continued, "has been sending Infernals after our Legacies for many centuries. One here, one there. Never has she tried to take so many at once. Now that we have a possible deadline, we need to move fast. The Legacies are no longer safe to live their lives among the ungifted humans."

"Mr. Bardin," Alicia Townsgate spoke next, "my condolences over your Guardian and your brother. You are a Gemini, yes? Losing that connection must be exceptionally difficult."

Damien's jaw clenched. "You want Amelia dealt with and I want to make her pay. Seems to me like we'll get along just fine, as long as you don't get in my way."

Townsgate shook her head. "Impertinent…" she said under her breath. "And you, Arianna March? is it vengeance you seek as well?"

"Who me?" I said with a nervous laugh. "I'm not a vengeance kind of gal." But even as I said this, I sobered. Recalling the heinous creature that came after me, I knew that anything capable of commanding that thing was just as ugly on the inside.

"Look, all I want to do is get my life back, go to university, be with my friends, but I realize as long as Amelia is free that will never happen. So however I can help I'm in."

She seemed to approve of this by way of a subtle nod.

"Is this the one, Abner?" she asked. "The Child on the Cusp?"

"It is," he said somberly.

"Ms. March, if you would please, we would like to see your Gift firsthand."

Professor Abner turned back to me and gave me a reassuring smile. He closed the gap between us and his dark eyes met mine. "It's going to be alright. Go ahead and show them."

Then he stepped aside to let me walk forward. I held my fists out, took a deep, steadying breath, and closed my eyes. When I opened my palms, I heard the anticipated gasp rise from the council members as they watched the illuminated constellations on my palms. An Aquarius on the right, a Pisces on the left.

"Dios Mio…" one of them said in awe.

When I finally looked up, I saw them whispering to each other, conferring over what they'd witnessed. I chanced a look at Damien, who was rolling his eyes. He clearly cared very little for bureaucracy.

"Abner…" Alicia finally spoke, "you are the Guardian of this Gifted?"

Ashley Kaplan

"I am."

"Very well. Her training is to start immediately. We will monitor her progress as you go along. For the moment, we must keep her gift a guarded secret. Once knowledge of her existence spreads, she won't be safe even within the walls of Astro City. If we know one thing to be true it is that Amelia will not stand for such a threat to exist. You are also to dispatch teams to assist any Guardian who needs to bring in their Legacies. I'm afraid none of us are safe anymore." She sighed heavily, the burden on her shoulders seeming a tangible thing. "The battle is at our doorstep. We must prepare the Astral Warriors."

*

In the days that followed, Professor Abner scheduled me for training sessions multiple times a day. Thanks to his subtle involvement in my childhood, I already had a basic knowledge of self-defense but not much in the way of fighting skills. Recalling the generosity of foster parents who sent me to self-defense classes, boxing lessons, martial arts, and yoga over the years, I had no idea at the time that Abner was playing puppet master behind the scenes. Funding these extracurricular activities, training me without my knowledge.

But facing an Infernal in real life was a different story and required a different type of concentration. Abner began working with me on my chi, the concept of harnessing my energies and concentrating them into a single force. I worked tirelessly on honing my skills as a cusp child, commanding air and water to my will. Well... trying to anyway. Air was easier; I was able to reach out and feel the pressure around me Water was tricky. No matter how much I tried, I couldn't get it to form to my will.

"You seemed to be able to command your powers in the alley," Abner accused me one day after a failed attempt.

"My life was on the line. I didn't exactly have any choice."

"Try it again."

Professor Abner pushed me day after day to harness my gifts. We would drive out to the desert some days to practice away from prying eyes. The fresh air and distance from the city relieved some of the pressure.

"Legends say that a Child on the Cusp could, theoretically, move mountains by sheer will," he said as he circled me, a stick in hand, as I stood blindfolded, listening to his footsteps. "You are connected to the elements thanks to the Zodiacs' gifts."

"How am I supposed to fight you if I can't see you?"

"You don't need to see me, Arianna. You are attuned to elements. Reach within you to your gift. Find it and take hold. Feel the ground move beneath my steps as I walk. Feel the air shift around you as my weapon moves towards you."

Ashley Kaplan

Snap.

I felt the sting of the stick hit my left arm and swung back at nothing.

"You are still trying to use your mundane senses," he said and I could almost hear the shake of his head. "Open yourself up to your new senses."

Snap.

Another hit landed on my thigh. I winced and swung around, getting tired of the bruising. "Don't you think this is bordering a little on child abuse?" I asked sarcastically.

Snap.

"Ow! Okay look, I know I'm not going to prom or anything but can we cool it with the bruising?"

Snap.

I spun my head around, trying to hear the shuffle of his feet over the pebbles. "Okay, stop it," my voice rose an octave. I was losing my patience with this sick little game.

Snap.

"Hey!"

Sna—

"Ooof!" I heard the weight of his body slam into the ground before he yelled out. I hadn't touched him but I knew this was my doing. It was there, right there at my fingertips. The power that everyone kept talking about and somehow I knew that I had only tapped into it. I felt its electricity humming on my skin. Ripping the blindfold off my face, I examined my hands and felt the flesh on my arms, and I realized what my trigger was.

Pain.

Just like at the Baru's cabin, when the pain from the Aqrab became too much, I was finally able to summon some sort of strength to fight it. Abner laying several feet away on the ground. He was wincing, his glasses askew, but he had a smile on his face that resembled pride.

"That's my girl," he said under his breath.

I couldn't help it, his smile was contagious and his pride encouraging. I could feel my gift. I could learn how to reach it.

I headed back to my room, feeling exhausted from a full day's workout. But even though I was tired, my body was buzzing. I had never summoned my power for such a long period.

Ashley Kaplan

For the first time since arriving at Astro City, it gave me hope that I could reach my potential, but I knew it was still a far cry from being able to stand against those horrifying creatures.

As I walked past the training rooms, a spinning movement caught my eyes. I stopped and walked over to the door, peeking through its window. Damien was in there, black t-shirt over dark jeans, gripping an axe and hurling it at a bullseye. I took a breath and pushed open the door.

"Am I interrupting?"

He looked at me through wisps of hair falling over his eyes and I had the distinct urge to brush them out of his face. I immediately chided myself for the ridiculous thought.

"No, it's cool. You can come in. You went out with Professor Abner today, right?"

I smiled. "Yeah, I'll be sore tomorrow morning but It was worth it. You're training?"

"Some people do yoga. I do this."

I walked over to him and grabbed hold of one of the weapons. Its weight felt comfortable in my hands. I stepped forward, pulled my arm back, and hurled it at the target. It hit several inches from the bullseye but close enough that I was satisfied. All those years of workouts did wonders for my hand, eye, coordination.

Damien came to stand beside me and grinned, folding his arms across his chest. "So what did you used to do for fun? In your other life?"

"Ha! Yeah, not a lot of time for fun when you're an orphan and have to pave your own way in the world. But I mean yeah, there were good times."

"You got friends you left behind?"

"Good ones," I said with a sad smile. "One of whom you met."

"So, what did you tell them?"

"Nothing, what could I say?" I shrugged. "Anyway, they're better off. In a job like this, it's better to keep them at a distance. Safe. At least until this is all over."

"Guess I can't argue with that," he said. "I've been remembering things. Bits and pieces, you know? Phillips taught my brother and me about this world. We grew up learning to fight and defend ourselves. We knew what those poor suckers out there are blind to. Monsters are real."

"That doesn't sound like a fun childhood," I said cautiously.

"Hey, I'd rather know what's really out there. He did us a favor. Phillips used to say we were 'in the life.' And when you're in the life of a Legacy, losing people kind of comes with the job."

He looked at me quietly for a moment then said, "I'm sorry Ari. I know this all took you by surprise. Maybe when this is all over you can get that life back."

I chuckled "I don't think you actually believe that any more than I do, but thank you anyway. Besides, I never truly felt like I was normal. I mean, I know everyone says that, but there was something in me that never felt quite finished. Like I wasn't me yet. Then when I got my apartment and started school, I finally felt like I was starting to figure it out. But... now that I know the truth... there's this whole new person I have to get to know."

"Well, whoever that person is, it looks like she's turning out to be kind of a badass Giftie."

He gave me a wink and walked away to retrieve the weapons. I felt my cheeks burning and smiled, hoping that he hadn't noticed. This blushing was starting to become an annoying habit around Damien.

Ashley Kaplan

Pisces
Aries
Taurus
Gemini
Cancer
Leo
Virgo
Libra
Scorpio
Sagittarius
Capricorn
Aquarius

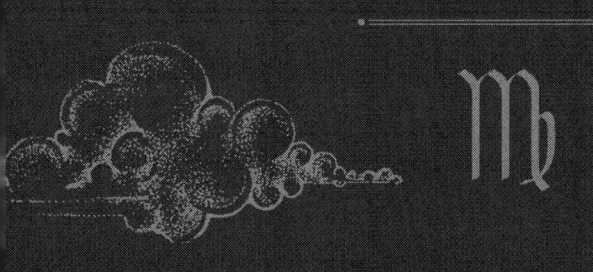

Heroics

"You can't rely only on your gift," Trinity, the weapons keeper, said to Damien and me in the armory. She looked like a delicate princess, small and thin with a fair complexion and thick blonde locks. Nobody would guess that she was as deadly as a viper if you put a weapon in her hands. She had the Gift of Scorpio and her power was clairvoyance. Trinity could predict the immediate future, which made her deadly in a fight.

"You have to hone your intuition. Infernals bleed and if it bleeds, you can kill it."

Damien swung around a battle axe, testing its weight and size. "Whatever, just point me at the thing and get out of my way."

Lifting one of the swords, I raised an eyebrow and looked at it quizzically. It felt heavier than I expected but I gripped the hilt with both hands and raised it. "I don't know if I'm a sword kind of girl, it clashes with my outfit."

Trinity grinned. "So does a bloody throat."

Damien shrugged. "Plus, you know, blood is a bitch to wash out your clothes."

Was he teasing me?

With a giggle, Trinity took the sword out of my hands and put it back in the weapons case. "I will ask Abner to go over some of these with you when he's done with Murphy."

"What are they up to?" I asked.

"Abner trains Murph, just like the rest of us."

"Isn't he a little young?"

She shrugged. "Sure, but he's a Legacy so Abner just wants him to be prepared."

Damien looked up from his weapon. "Wait, little dude's a Legacy? so his…?"

"His dad," she answered, "a Virgo."

It was my turn to act surprised. "Woah, Abner?"

Ashley Kaplan

"Oh no," Trinity shook her head. "Murphy's biological father was. They lost Jenna to cancer," she sighed, talking about who I assumed was Murphy's mom.

"His biological dad brought him to Astro City to raise but he was killed on a mission.

Professor Abner was good friends with Murphy's parents, so he adopted Murph after that and you know the rest."

"Poor Murphy," I said. I knew how it felt to lose both parents. "But why didn't Abner move to Astro with him, where it's safe?" I asked.

Trinity's brows tilted in a look of subtle confusion and her lips turned into a sympathetic smile.

"It was for you," she said gently.

Those words made me feel like an idiot. Abner brought Murphy back home with him so he could be a father and remain my Guardian. He could have abandoned me but he didn't. It occurred to me for the first time then just how much Abner had always been there for me, even before I knew it. On the sidelines but always watching and keeping close. Without my knowing, it was like I had a real family all along.

On the days that I wasn't training with Abner, Damien and I were learning more and more about the legends of the Zodiacs and the many other creatures in our world. Mostly we would hang out with Winifred on trips past the city walls into the mountains. Winifred was a Taurus and everyone just called her Fred for short. Her powers allowed her to manipulate people's emotions and soothe them into submission or relaxation. Although Winifred had lived in Astro for most of her life, she still had a hint of a Scottish accent and every so often dropped a word I couldn't understand. That morning her curly red hair bounced as she waved and she offered me a bright smile; something she never lacked was exuberance.

Farther into the mountains there were regions that were still forested, and streams trickled down the mountainside. This is where I would try and sharpen my water manipulation. Fred used her gift to calm me which helped me to focus. Only then was I truly able to manipulate the movements of the water. No matter how much I tried, air was so much easier for me to get a grip on than water. I couldn't see it in my mind, couldn't reach the gift within, to call it forth and use it at will.

"Don't get in your own head," she said one day on the mountain.

"I just can't reach my gift. Not properly," I said in frustration.

"You just need to practice. It will come to you in time. My powers used to be all over the place. It took me a long time to learn to control them, to steady my emotions so that I could manipulate others."

"I wish I could do that, there's a gift that would come in handy."

Ashley Kaplan

Fred laughed. The sound was like bird song, lovely and infectious. "You'd be surprised. Come on, let's go further up the mountain. Maybe you'll feel inspired."

We started heading further up along the river bed and farther up the mountain. The air was pristine out here, pure. The mountains hadn't suffered as much devastation from the Zodiac's absence as the rest of the world. I was reveling in the peacefulness when Winifred paused and held a hand up to stop me. The silence stretched as I quietly watched her concentrated features, waiting for something to come. I wanted to ask her why we had stopped but through the trees came an impossibly large creature by way of an answer. Then following behind him was another, and another, until there were five of them standing between the trunks, and watching us curiously.

They stood on cloven hooves, their bottom halves that of a bovine, with tails that flicked up and swatted at the air. Their torso was human, bare-chested, with wide shoulders and strong arms. But their heads were very clearly those of bulls, with large horns sticking out of their crowns. I gasped and took a step back, half in shock and half panic. There were five of them and only two of us, plus I was pretty sure I would be useless to Fred in a fight against these guys. But when I looked at her, Fred's face cleared into a calm demeanor and she waved her hand slowly at the creatures. They looked at her curiously, then seemed to study me, and with a sudden exhale through their nostrils, they turned and sprinted up the mountain with impossible speed, leaving me in stunned silence.

"It might be best if we called it a day," Winifred said to me with a gentle smile and a shrug.

"What? What were those things?" I asked slightly alarmed.

"Minotaurs. They pretty much own the mountains here and they can be a little territorial. I don't suggest coming up here on your own," she warned.

"Why didn't they attack us?"

Fred grinned. "Yo," she said and pointed to herself. "There used to be a faction of humans who worshiped Taurus back in his glory days. The Zodiac offered them eternal life and strength in exchange for their fealty, and they accepted. That's how the minotaurs came to be into existence. Because I have the gift of Taurus, they usually steer clear of me or any others from my sign. They respect the god's chosen heroes."

"But I'm...?"

"Fair game, yup!" She patted me on the back. "Don't be upset, I'm sure they think you're cool too." She winked at me with a smile. I had to smile back. I could tell I was going to really get along with Fred.

Weapons training and controlling my emotions were hard enough but the rest of the time the council insisted that Damien and I join Calypso and Orion on retrieval missions. They wanted me ready in the field and to take out as many Infernals as I could before I faced down Amelia. It was understood that it had to be me. Was *going* to be me to destroy the Cursed One. We were searching out locations of other Legacies. The word had spread far and wide and many Guardians and their wards had gone into hiding. Sometimes it felt like it didn't matter to the council what would happen to me in the process, as long as Amelia was stopped. On some sick level, I had to admit that I agreed with them. Not that I was a morbid person, but I was actually pretty happy with where my life was going before all of this. But there were things I couldn't look past. Body counts that were beginning to rise. I knew somewhere deep inside me that if I had to go down to take out Amelia then that was a sacrifice I had to make.

Each time we left Astro City, I could see Damien's determination grow, his need for vengeance was overwhelming. I couldn't say I blamed him. If I knew I had a family and a home that was all taken away from me just for existing, I would feel the same way. Still, as time went by, Damien began to loosen up a little, and even show some humor. Like when he was riding his bike, talking about his bike – basically anything to do with his bike put him in a good mood. I had to admit that a smile was a good look for him. He came off almost mischievous and I wondered, not for the first time, what he was like before this whole ordeal. I knew that some of his memories had been coming back and that bike was the only thing he had left of home. Damien had restored it with his brother and his Guardian, and he was going to ride it to his death if Amelia was at the end of that road.

We spent a lot of time with Calypso and Orion and it was easy to see the friendship that the two had formed was based on years of relying on each other and having each other's back. They laughed, teasing and making jokes which put me at ease around them. Despite that, though, I knew they still watched me carefully. Like at any moment I could explode or something. It made me realize that even surrounded by so many people, I was still completely alone. I figured that nobody knew what to make of me, how to treat me, except Damien. He didn't give a rat's ass that I was a cusp child.

I hated that title – the Child on the Cusp. But with each mission, Calypso and Orion tried to push me a little more. Encouraged me to trust my instincts and not rely on my growing powers. Powers that I was beginning to get a very cool grip on. The more I learned, the closer I was to taking Amelia down. The thought that other Legacies, other kids, were being hunted down like animals at her command gave me a renewed sense of purpose. Kids like Jono Lee.

"Twelve year old Jono Lee and his parents immigrated here from out East," Abner began in a briefing one morning to Damien, Calypso, Orion, and me. "What we found curious is while out on patrol we caught an Infernal sniffing around their home. The creature had climbed into the bedroom window of the youngest Lee and was… well it was sniffing his scent. Normally they would ransack the place but this was methodical, almost as though it found his scent somehow familiar."

Calypso shook her head. "What would make an Infernal do that?"

"Well, we're not quite sure. To be safe we had Tracy placed near the family to keep watch until we knew more."

"Alex's sister right?" I asked. "Are there Legacies that are that far out in the world?"

Abner looked thoughtful. "None that we know of. Your powers are linked to our Zodiacs. They aren't recognized in that part of the world and I should wonder how well they would even work if the link is so weakened by distance."

"Either way," I said, "this kid definitely piqued their interest."

"That's why I called you all here. Tracy didn't check in yesterday," Abner explained. "We can't get a hold of her but with the recent attacks, nothing can be left to chance."

"Just shoot over an address and we're on our way," said Orion.

So the team and I found ourselves outside an abandoned meat packing warehouse. This was supposedly Tracy's last known location before contact ended. We had stood outside the warehouse for too long, waiting for Orion to scope out the place.

"What the hell is taking so long?" Damien said impatiently.

"Orion knows what he's doing. We're all eager to get Jono and Tracy back to safety but we have to do this right," said Calypso.

"What do we do if they're not here?" I asked.

"One problem at a time," she said calmly but I could see the nervous edge to her in the way she tensed up.

Then Orion appeared from around the corner. "Alright, no sign of anything unusual that I can see from out here. We'll have to go in deeper."

"Great," said Damien, "let's get this show on the road."

He tightened his grip on his weapon of choice, the battle axe, and led the way into the warehouse. Damien had been working on harnessing his gift with Calypso, just like I was with Abner, but he nearly always chose the axe over the use of his powers. It was almost like he preferred close combat. But that seemed to fit with who he was; a 'shoot first ask questions later,' kind of guy. I decided to go with the much simpler and easy-to-handle dagger. About the size of my forearm, it was light and quick and I could aim it easily.

We entered the building on high alert and cautiously started to scout out the main floor. Everything was rubble and dirt – empty with no sign of Tracy or Jono Lee so far.

"This could take a while. I think we need to split up," I said. The thought of the Infernals still gave me major creeps. But the idea of this little boy hiding somewhere trumped that.

"She's right," Calypso agreed. "Orion and I will check upstairs."

I nodded. "We can clear the ground floor."

They turned and made their way up the stairs as Damien and I headed further into the warehouse. I clenched my fists and tested out the feel of the fingerless gloves that Abner had instructed me to wear. He didn't want the star signs on my palms to give away what I was.

"If you wanted to be alone with me, you could have just said so," Damien smirked.

"Yeah, that was my big plan. Nothing screams romance like a rat-infested building."

"Who said anything about romance?"

I rolled my eyes. "Jono Lee is my priority right now. Anyway, what happened to the angry and brooding guy I met?"

"Oh, I'm still angry and plenty brooding."

"Mhm, I thought all you cared about was finding Amelia and taking her out."

Damien paused and clenched his jaw. "Look, Ari, we will find Amelia eventually," he said, no nonsense. "But until then we're going to take out as many Infernals as we can to even the score."

I sighed. "It just seems like they keep coming. Legacy after Legacy are disappearing and how many have we managed to save? How many Guardians have we seen hurt or dead?"

"Hey, you can't put that on yourself. We do the job and save as many people as we can."

"And the ones we can't save?"

"We avenge. One less Infernal on the streets is a win in my book."

We both heard the noise at the same time as we rounded the corner and raised our weapons.

"Woah, woah!"

The guy on the other side was pointing a rifle at us. He immediately lowered it and raised a hand in surrender. The other, I noticed, was still clutching the firearm. He looked to be middle-aged, wearing a baseball cap, a long-sleeved shirt under a hunting vest with faded jeans and black boots. What was he doing here?

"You have ten seconds to explain yourself," I said.

"I'm just looking for my friend, alright? Last I heard from her, she was coming here."

Damien and I exchanged skeptical looks.

"Who's this friend?" Damien asked.

"Look, her name is Tracy and I think she's in trouble. Now can we all just put down our weapons?"

Damien nodded at his rifle. "You first, buddy."

The stranger smiled and slowly lowered his rifle to hang off his shoulder at his side.

"Alright?" he asked.

Damien and I lowered our weapons, cautiously.

"What's your name?" I asked him.

"Edgar. And you folks are?"

"I'm Damien, this is Ari. How do you know Tracy?"

"She's my neighbor."

"We're looking for her too," I said. "We... we work with her."

Edgar looked surprised. "You two? Work at the coffee shop?"

I looked at the dagger still in my hand and quickly sheathed it. "Oh, this? Well, we work in a bad neighborhood."

"Mhm, super bad" Damien said sarcastically.

"Lots of break-ins and... you know... those damn teenagers."

"Yup, we're especially afraid of the teenagers," Damien agreed.

"Oh, I thought you guys were here because those scary as hell creatures were after her." He fixed the cap on his head. "Guess I was wrong."

Damien looked at me with an annoyed glare, probably for making him go along with such a stupid lie.

"Yeah, that too," he said.

"Wait you saw them?" I asked.

"Well, yeah. A few nights ago one was sniffing around the Lee residence. Saw him when I was coming home from work. Couldn't believe my damn eyes. Thing attacked me. I'd be worm food if it wasn't for Tracy. Turned that thing into a puddle."

"What makes you think she's here?"

"She left me a message saying she needed help and where to find her. Figured it was something serious so I brought some backup," He patted his rifle to indicate. "Was just about to check the basement when I ran into you two."

I glanced at Damien, who shrugged. "Alright, lead the way," he said roughly.

Edgar gave us a weak smile but obliged, leading us to the basement door. The heavy metal screeched from years of neglect as it swung open and we took the stairs down. The lights were dimmer down there and the hallways narrow but eventually we reached a set of double doors. Edgar swung them open and sauntered in. Even though Damien and I were only steps away, by the time we entered, Edgar was gone. We were in a large lab, although it was pretty much empty, there were mostly long metal tables in rows.

"Son of a bitch! Where did he go?" Damien whispered.

There was a door to our left and one to our right, Edgar could have gone through either of them. "Split up," I said and Damien took my cue, his weapon in hand. He went right and I hung a left. Dagger in hand, I pushed the door open slowly. The fluorescent lights flickered as I passed by more metal tables. It was eerily quiet and the hairs on the back of my neck stood up as goosebumps ran down my arms, suddenly overtaken by an inexplicable cold. I heard slow footsteps behind and turned, hoping to find Damien, but instead came face-to-face with an apparition. It was a girl, the same one I had seen at the Baru's house, I was sure of it. She looked to be around my age, with golden brown skin and dark hair. Dressed in battle gear, she looked like she was from another century and with a sense of confidence that was unmistakable.

"Hey Giftie," she said quietly.

"I know you," I said, now remembering her face clear as day. "You were there at the Baru's house. I saw you outside the window."

"And I saw you." Her lips curved up in a half smile.

"You sent the Aqrab after us, didn't you? You're one of Amelia's cursed humans."

"Quick one, aren't ya? Good for you, they must have you taking your vitamins at Astro."

"Who are you?" I demanded, my dagger raised and ready to fight.

"I'm Imani, but I think the real question is who are you?" she said with a twinkle in her eye. "Why don't you take those pretty little gloves off and we can clear all this up."

"My gloves?" I asked, confused. I wasn't prepared for her to ask me about those. Nobody outside my team and the Council knew about my gifts.

"It's no big deal, just a little peek at those delicate hands," Imani said.

"If this is your super weird way of coming on to me, I gotta tell ya, you're not my type." I glared at her.

"I'm everyone's type," she said with a wink, "but you're not that lucky. Now be a good little Giftie and take off your gloves."

"First of all, the name is Ari. If you're going to be creepy, at least get it right. Second of all, and this is the most important thing… screw you hell bitch."

Ashley Kaplan

"I was hoping you'd say that."

My instincts kicked in before her fist did and I dodged her attack. She kept coming at me and Imani was fast. I couldn't fight her, only deflect her blows as I backed up. She swung again and this time I raised my dagger and slashed her across the palm. When she snapped her hand back and hissed in pain, I used her distraction to connect my fist with her jaw. She snapped back with a rejoinder and I was hurled down against a metal table, the wind knocked out of me. Sheathing my right dagger, with my left I swung back but Imani grabbed my wrist and twisted, the pain spreading up my arm and making me yell out. The dagger slipped to the floor as she pinned me down and I could feel her fighting the glove off my hand.

"Well hey there, Aquarius," she said. "Let's take a look at the other one shall we?"

My mind raced in a panic when I realized she was going to uncover my secret. Using my foot to push away from the table, I felt Imani stumble backward as my body weight slammed into her. I swung my head back as hard as I could and headbutted her. It worked and my hand was freed from her grasp. I turned around and kneed her in the stomach for good measure before bending down to snatch up my dagger. Imani's reflexes were quick and as I bent down, she grabbed me by the hair and slammed my face into the table edge. The metallic taste of blood assaulted my taste buds. I raised the hand holding the dagger and forced it into Imani's leg. She screamed and almost threw me away from he as she clutched onto her bleeding thigh. I didn't waste a minute and hurled myself at the door, running out of the room as Imani screamed in outrage behind me. Through the double doors I kept going down the hallways until I ran straight into a hard body and raised my dagger in the air.

"Woah, woah! Ari, it's me! It's Damien."

"Damien..." I panted, my chest heaving. I noticed he had found Edgar after all.

"We have to find Orion and Calypso. There's someone here—"

All three of us looked up when we heard the scream, immediately followed by a loud bang.

"You good to do this?"

I wasn't sure if I was but with the intense look in his eye and him to back me up, I nodded somberly.

"Help or stay out of the way," Damien told Edgar.

Running up the stairs and down the stone halls, I could hear the commotion even louder now. My heart was in my throat; I knew a fight was coming. We burst into a wide, empty floor with a few desks and chairs still sitting around. Orion was standing in a black puddle of what used to be an Infernal but there was another one standing right above him atop a work desk, drool seeping from its mouth, ready to devour him.

Ashley Kaplan

Calypso was also covered in black splatter, lying flat on her back, but an Infernal had its claws over her hands. She squirmed and I could see the panic in her eyes now that she couldn't use her powers or reach her weapons.

Behind me, Edgar raised his rifle. "There's another one coming up them stairs," he said. "I'll cover you. Go help your friends."

Damien and I sprang into action. He went for Orion and I for Calypso. I stopped just feet away, grabbed a stone off the ground, and hurled the thing as hard as I could with a little extra Gifted force. It hit the beast squarely between the shoulders. The distraction worked; it turned away from Calypso and stared me down, drool pooling at its feet as a low growl escaped its throat.

"Okay look," I said. "We can do this the hard way or—" I ducked and dropped down as a chair came hurtling at me. Getting back up I turned to the Infernal. "Hard way. Got it."

The creature balled its massive hands over Calypso's effortlessly and I heard her cry out in pain. When he let go and stood up, she rolled over, covering her now damaged hands.

"That was a big mistake," I said, anger rising inside me like a tidal wave.

The creature began to charge at me, closing the gap between us it swung its hand at me. I dodged it but the other hand was just as fast and its claws cut straight across my rib cage, a stinging pain shooting through my body. Hissing I stumbled backward, but the creature didn't give me a chance to recover. It darted forward and with Abner's words echoing in my memory I felt the air from the movement it made. With a swipe of my hand, I compressed it and pushed the force back into him, throwing his arms far back, leaving his midsection wide open. I raised my leg and planted it firmly in his chest, pushing.

The Infernal stumbled backward and bared its teeth, growling. Swinging its tail, the creature swiftly knocked me to the ground but my reflexes were working on overdrive. I rolled over, just missing its claws as they dug into the floor where my head had been seconds ago. Sliding my dagger out, I stabbed it right in the ankle and heard the roar in pain. Rolling out of the way, I got back to my feet, and my hands immediately twisted in a circular motion while he was distracted. I heard Abner's reassuring words in my head, telling me to feel the air around me and the earth beneath me.

Just past the creature, I could see Orion and Damien fighting off an Infernal. To my left, I saw Edgar firing off shots, holding back the other one that was trying to get up to our floor. Calypso still lay wounded and defenseless.

The tidal wave within me had reached its peak and was going to swallow that creature whole until there was nothing left. It raced at me full force but time felt like it had slowed to me. The little stones on the ground began to quiver and shake as they rose from the air. I pushed my arms back and, with a deep breath, pushed forward. The pebbles shot at the Infernal all at once, at such a speed that for a moment I lost track of them.

The creature stopped, disoriented. It looked down at its chest where blotches of black ink began to form and I realized the stones had gone right through. Staring in shock, I watched as the creature burst into a puddle of inky black goo.

"Woah..."

I looked at my hands, in awe of what I had just done. I had no idea I was capable of something like that, but my mind snapped back to reality. Running to Calypso, I dropped to my knees beside her.

"Hey, Caly look at me, are you ok? How are your hands?"

The pain in her eyes was unmistakable as tears gathered at their corners. "I'll be fine but, Ari, we have to get out of here."

"I hear you. Can you walk?" She nodded and I helped her to her feet. She held her mangled hands close to her chest.

Edgar fired off another warning shot. "I'm thinkin' we best be getting on our way folks."

Damien and Orion closed the space between us and Orion seemed particularly disturbed. The Infernal they had fought had been reduced to nothing.

"Caly, your hands!" he said, alarmed.

"Not to beat a dead horse but there's more'n one of them coming up here," said Edgar.

"Calypso is in no shape to fight," I said. "Get her to the van and I'll hold them back."

"NO!"

"Are you crazy?"

Orion and Calypso spoke in unison and I wasn't sure who said what.

"We don't have time for this," I insisted. "Get the hell out of here."

"You three go," Damien said. "We'll be right behind you."

Orion shook his head. "We can't."

Just then we heard the rattling of the metal staircase. It nearly shook the floor with its force.

"She can't fight, Orion," I said. "Go."

He hesitated, unsure of what to do, but finally, he nodded and grabbed Calypso by the arm. The three of them left and Damien and I stood alone, shielding them with our bodies.

"Any bright ideas?" he asked.

I palmed the dagger in my hand and raised it. "Kill everyone?"

"Okay, yeah. I like that plan."

"Thought you might," I said, near breathless.

We braced ourselves to face off the creatures but as the Infernal finally made it up the stairs and over the rail what followed behind it made my heart race in a panic. Wide eyed, I stared at another Aqrab, much larger than the last. This time we didn't have the benefit of fire to help fend it off.

"Oh crap," Damien said.

"Damien, we can't fight that thing."

We both knew taking the Aqrab down would be too difficult one-on-one. It would be even harder with an Infernal on its heels, protecting it. After that, there was no time to think. The two creatures had us dead in their sights, advancing on us.

I wasn't sure how much good my rock trick would do against the Aqrab, with its brick-like shell and his tail acting as a shield. His chest was vulnerable but I was wary of getting close to him.

"I hope I live to regret this…" I mumbled.

Crouching down, I broke into a run, straight at the Aqrab. Inches away from him ,I lowered my body to the ground and slid across the floor right under his scorpion body. I felt the burn from the open wound on my ribs as my body stretched and rubbed against the stone. It was a terrifying few seconds as I made it to the other side and flung both my daggers backward, willing the gift of Aquarius to make my aim true.

They embedded themselves between the beast's shoulder blades and he screamed out in anger, rather than pain. As he squirmed, trying to pull the weapons out of his back, I got to my feet and ran around him to Damien, who was deflecting blows with his axe. Without thinking, I jumped high up onto the Infernal's back and wrapped my legs around him and my arms around his neck. He went stumbling back and slammed into the wall, with me still on his back, knocking the wind out of me.

Damien charged him and slammed his shoulder in the thing's gut. The Aqrab swung his tail and knocked Damien off his feet, and reached his arms to me. The Infernal dug his claws in my back and pulled me forward over his head, landing me hard on the floor. Just as I turned over to face him, I saw that the Infernal was now on top of me. Damien got to his feet, pulled his arm back, and hurled the axe as hard as he could.

It hit the target on the top of his head and I watched the creature's body go limp and topple before he turned into a puddle. Retrieving Damien's axe, I forced myself to push forward and ran over, grabbing him by the arm.

"We have to go, come on!"

"But the Aqrab…"

Ashley Kaplan

The beast was getting frustrated with its futile attempt to get at the daggers and turned a seething stare on us.

"COME ON!" I shouted as I pushed Damien towards the stairs.

He didn't argue after that, neither one of us was prepared to fight that thing. It screamed in a horrific high-pitched voice as it came after us. Damien turned back to look at it; I was just steps ahead of him. Then suddenly he picked up speed and grabbed me around my legs, lifting me and kept running.

"What the hell?!" I yelled.

"Cover us!" he shouted. "Make it a little harder for him would you?" he panted as he ran. I clued in to what he was thinking and turned in his arms as he ran.

Using all my concentration, I spread my arms and willed the air around me to bend and push. Immediately, work desks scratched across the floor as they began to move and desk chairs flew into the air, hurtling at the Aqrab.

Stones, office furniture, leftover staplers, anything that wasn't weighed down was flying at its body. Damien finally burst through the doors and set me down. His bike was right there and we wasted no time getting on it. The sound of the bike revving up was like music to my ears as the Aqrab burst through the doors. We weren't fast enough and I braced myself for another fight when gunshots gave it pause.

Orion was in the car across the lot, waiting for us, Edgar hanging out the window. I gave Orion the most appreciative smile I had ever felt as Damien sped us away from the warehouse, Orion just on our heels, leaving the creature in our dust.

As soon as we got back, Alex and Jonah were waiting for us in the entry hall. Alex's usual spark and mischievous grin were gone, replaced by worry lines.

"Well?" he asked. "What happened?"

I shook my head, apologetically. "There was nobody there. We were ambushed."

A fire ignited in his sea blue eyes; a wave of impotent anger that he couldn't release.

"Woah, Caly!" Jonah said wide-eyed. "Your hands are all messed up."

Damien gave the kid an annoyed look and smacked him on the back of the head for his insensitive remark.

"Yeah, they are," he said, "so maybe you should take her to see the doctor."

Jonah blushed and nodded, escorting Calypso out of there.

"Alex, this is Edgar," I said. "He's a friend of Tracy's. We ran into him at the warehouse. He was also looking for her."

"You know my sister?" Alex asked.

Edgar smiled. "She saved my life."

"Alex," Orion started, "why don't you take Edgar somewhere he can relax and wait for us. Abner will want to meet him."

Alex gave me a sharp look, obviously displeased at playing chaperone but he didn't argue. He grunted and walked away, leaving Edgar to follow.

I offered him a weak smile but something didn't sit right with me. The rest of us headed straight to the war room to wait for Calypso, who returned later with Abner at her side. Her hands were bandaged up with something similar to a cast but of a much softer material. Later I would be told that it was Dr. Levine's invention to help Gifteds' wounds heal.

"Welcome back everyone," Abner said in his usually calm voice. "Now I know we're all worried about Tracy and young Mr. Lee. And we have to deal with our visitor as well—"

"We're all on the jump here though right?" I interrupted. "Edgar? He's a bad guy. That was obviously a trap, right?"

"Now, we can't jump to any conclusions here."

"Sure, sure," I nodded. "Um, question?"

Abner sighed, exasperated. "Yes, Arianna?"

"What about taking a leisurely stroll to conclusions? Because however we get there, you know, fine by me," I said with a shrug.

"I'm with Cuspy over there," said Damien. "Somethin' don't smell right with that guy."

"Cuspy?" I asked horrified.

"You're not kidding," Orion grimaced.

"Cuspy?!" I repeated, high-pitched. "When did we decide on that nickname?"

"I think it's kind of on the nose," Calypso said, holding back a laugh.

"I know, right?" Damien grinned.

"Children please!" Abner raised his voice, not quite a yell but it got our attention. "This is serious. We can't take anything for granted here. There is a little boy and one of our own who are missing. Now if you believe our guest had something to do with that then it's a good thing you brought him in. At least now we can question him properly and detain him if needed. This isn't the time to be making jokes and speculating. We're going to bring

Edgar in for questioning. In the meantime, Orion, get your ear to the ground and see if you can come up with any leads. Witnesses, anything that might help locate Tracy and the boy. Now, are you all ready to get to work?"

We all looked dutifully ashamed after that scolding. Orion was the first to speak and hopped up to his feet.

"I'm on it, Professor," he said.

Calypso cleared her throat. "I'll go get Edgar and bring him to the interrogation room." She nudged Damien. "Come on, I could use some help."

Even Damien looked appropriately ashamed. "Yup, let's go."

Then it was just Abner and I left alone in the war room. He had turned his back on me and was sifting through some paperwork. There was too much on my mind since I had learned about Murphy and this was the first time I had been alone with Abner since finding out. I knew I had to address it. There was so much I wanted to say to him but I didn't know where to start,

"Hey, Abner?" I started slowly. "I heard about Murphy. I mean, that he's a Legacy."

His body tensed briefly and then his shoulders slumped. He turned around with a sigh and leaned back against the table, rubbing the bridge of his nose in that familiar way of his that implied he was tired.

"Then I suppose you also know he's not my biological son."

"Yeah, that too."

"Well yes. Murphy is not related to me by blood, but he is my son."

"No, I know. I mean, I've seen," I was fumbling my words. "You're a great dad to him."

Abner looked at me, no doubt trying to figure out what my point was. "Look," I said, "I know you could have stayed here with him to continue his training. To protect him better. That you could have sent another Guardian to watch over me. I guess I wanted to know why you didn't?"

Abner was silent for a moment as though he was attempting to understand my question. "Why I didn't? Arianna… you have been my responsibility since you were a child."

"Responsibility. Right. Okay, yes, I get it."

"No, I don't quite think that you do," he said, shaking his head. "I have watched from the sidelines as you grew up from a frightened and confused child into a confident and inspiring young woman. You took advantage of every opportunity that was given to you, worked hard, and persevered."

"Well, that's flattering Abner, but you weren't just watching on the sidelines. You practically funded my entire childhood without my knowing. Why?"

"Because I knew you were meant to be a great hero one day. And it was a privilege to watch you become the leader that I am seeing before me today."

"So you stuck around to watch your investment pay out."

"I stuck around, as you put it, because I was very proud of you and all you accomplished, and I still am."

I felt the last strands of bitterness and doubt melt away, finally allowing myself to do what I had been afraid to ever since I stepped foot into Astro City – trust Davy Abner again.

Looking back at my childhood I realized that I could have had it so much worse. Ended up with horrible families or even out on the street. But Abner was always there behind the scenes, manipulating the situation. He protected me, prepared me, and ensured that I was placed in the best homes. Thanks to him I didn't end up bitter and forgotten about.

"So you came back for me. I guess I'm kind of okay with that," I said with a smile.

Abner smiled back, the gesture reaching his eyes. "I'm glad to hear it, Ms. March."

Ashley Kaplan

Aries
Taurus
Gemini
Cancer
Leo
Virgo
Libra
Scorpio
Sagittarius
Capricorn
Aquarius
Pisces

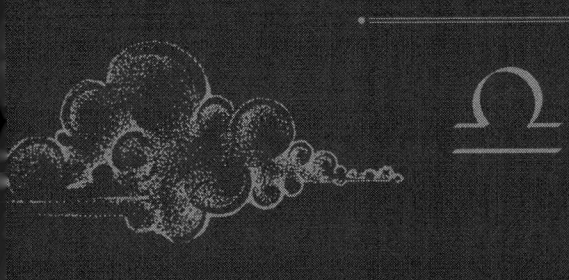

Forgiving

We stood outside the interrogation room where Edgar sat waiting.

"Alright, who's going in?" asked Calypso.

"Give me a beat with him," said Damien and took a menacing step forward. Orion put a hand out to stop him.

"The guy can't tell us anything if he's unconscious."

"I'll go," I said confidently. Nobody argued and Calypso nodded.

"I'll join you," Abner offered and stepped forward, holding the door open for me.

Edgar was sitting down, elbows on the table, twiddling his thumbs. "Hey guys, been waitin' for you. What's going on?"

Abner walked around and took a seat across from him while I remained standing.

"Look," I spoke slowly. "My friend is missing and so is a little boy, so we're just going to cut to the chase. What do you know about their disappearance?"

Edgar seemed surprised. "Wait a minute, you don't think I had something to do with that, do you?"

I rolled my eyes. "Well let's see. Tracy has never mentioned you in her correspondence, has she, Abner?"

"I don't believe she has."

"And you just happened to be at the warehouse where she conveniently went missing, and oh right! Where we were ambushed."

"I was just there to help. Like I said."

Something in his eyes gave him away; a sparkle that came from the hint of a smirk and made my blood boil. I wasn't going to lose somebody else to Amelia. Certainly not a helpless little boy who was innocent in all of this. Stepping forward, I raised my arm ready to attack but, within moments, Abner laid a gentle hand over mine and gave me pause.

"Edgar is it? Listen, you seem like a capable guy. Surely you know where this is going."

Maybe it was the calmness in Abner's voice, or maybe how sure he sounded, but for the first time, Edgar looked alarmed. His eyes darted back and forth between Abner and me. He seemed to be thinking out his options but sat back and crossed his arms over his chest.

"You can't make me talk."

"I rather like to believe I can," Abner countered.

"You ever heard the saying, 'You can catch more bees with honey'?"

"Certainly, that's why I kept Arianna from breaking your nose... for now."

There was that look of alarm again and I had to give it to Abner; he knew how to make a guy nervous.

"That's the honey," I said. "What was the other part of that saying? Something about vinegar?"

"You think you can scare me?" Edgar said, raising his voice.

"Um yeah, I think I can," I said. "Shall I try?"

"Whatever you do to me won't matter. She already knows everything she needs to."

I raised an eyebrow. "She?"

"You are referring to Amelia, I take it?" Abner asked.

Edgar sat back in his chair, fidgeting in his seat, clearly uncomfortable at the mention of Amelia.

"Know *what*, Edgar? You don't have to be afraid of her here, we can protect you."

"Protect me?" he asked with a chuckle. "You won't even be able to protect yourselves. No, I'm not scared. Oh, but you should be, girlie."

Abner narrowed his eyes. "What exactly is that supposed to mean?"

Edgar leaned over the table so that he was close to Abner and his lips curved into a twisted smirk. "You should have known that you couldn't keep her a secret forever," he whispered.

Abner avoided looking at me, but I could see his entire body tense with Edgar's warning.

"I don't know what you mean," he said simply.

Edgar threw his head back and laughed cruelly. "You can try and deny it all you want, but we know about the cusp sign. Seeing her in action was... disappointing."

My heart began to drum loudly in my chest. Here was the confirmation of my worst fear. We had lost the element of surprise and Amelia knew of my existence. What did that mean for me now? For any of us?

"I see, so Tracy was simply the bait to draw out some imaginary warrior you think is in our ranks?"

"Tracy was a casualty, way in over her head. I would worry less about her and more about saving your sorry hides. Death will be resurrected, you are too late."

"What?" Those words echoed in the room as they did in my dream.

"Amelia will bathe in the blood of your precious gods," Edgar smirked cruelly.

I stepped back from Edgar as though his words burned me. Things were coming together in my head and suddenly I understood what had been plaguing me for so many weeks.

"Abner? A word please."

I pushed him out of the room and snapped the door shut behind me.

"We have to talk. Get Argus, get the team. I think I may have some answers."

Taking a deep breath, I braced myself, standing in the war room with Abner, Damien, Calypso, Orion, and Argus. I knew this was going to sound unbelievable but so far none of this seemed real. What was a little more crazy thrown into the mix?

"First off, I think it's safe to say Amelia knows a cusp sign is officially a player on the board."

Abner nodded. "The council had hoped our enemies would think you were just another Gifted, they wanted to send you out on missions to give you valuable field experience. I'm afraid now though we have to operate on the assumption that Amelia does indeed know your true nature."

"How the hell did they figure that out?" Damien asked with an aggressive undertone.

"That does seem to be the question of the hour," Abner said. "Only very few people here know about her."

"So all of us, and those council members who we barely know," Damien said pointedly.

"Are you implying it was one of them?" Calypso asked, surprised.

"That's where I would start looking," he said.

Abner shook his head. "I don't believe that is likely, but we can't rule anyone out at this point."

"Look," I went on, "I would love to know how Amelia found out my true powers and although we should definitely figure that out, we knew this was a possibility. I say for now we concentrate on a problem we can solve. Edgar said that 'death will resurrect' but the thing is I've heard that before. What the little weasel didn't realize is that I know the end of that sentence."

"What do you mean?" asked Abner.

"'Death will resurrect where new life is given; a dip in the wrong hands will summon the vision.'"

"Where did you hear that?"

"This is the part you might find hard to believe," I exhaled slowly. "Aquarius told me… in a dream."

"Aquarius told you?" Orion asked skeptically.

"The Zodiac?" Abner clarified.

"One and the same," I said confidently.

"*The* Aquarius?" Abner asked in disbelief. "I'm afraid you'll have to elaborate."

"I can't explain it, Abner; I've been having dreams where I meet with her in some sort of in-between worlds place. I don't know. She keeps telling me to 'find it' but she's never told me what *it* is. The dreams are sporadic but in the last one, she said to me 'death will resurrect where new life is given.' Whatever it is she wants me to find, Amelia is looking for it also, I'm sure of it. And Abner, she was scared. I mean the thought of Amelia getting her hands on this thing scared a Zodiac."

There was a stunned silence in the room. Only Abner pulled himself together to speak.

"What makes you so sure she was afraid?"

"We know that during the Observation of the Ascendant, Amelia can open a door to the Zodiacs' realm. She's going to attack them and Aquarius knows it. She told me 'Our enemies will bathe in all our blood.' I thought she meant us, the Gifted, but when Edgar just repeated it, I realized she meant herself and the other Zodiacs. Whatever this thing is, it must be powerful enough to hurt them."

"Heaven help us all," Calypso whispered.

Damien, who had been quiet this whole time, came to stand beside me. "Okay, so the next question is what could be so powerful that would scare a god?"

"Is there anything else you can recall?" Abner urged.

I tried to think back on our conversations, but they were so fragmented and strange that it was hard to pick out the one thing that could mean something.

"Oh! yes! Whatever this thing is, she said that she lost it in the Great Fall."

Abner looked thoughtful for a moment and then stalked purposefully over to the bookshelves. He retrieved a brown leather-bound title and flipped through it as he returned then slammed the open book down on the table. Argus looked over the pages and his expression changed from curious to awed.

"You truly think...?" he left the question unfinished.

"I'm afraid so," Abner said.

Damien cleared his throat. "Hey, old guys, want to share with the group?"

Abner gave him a disapproving glare. "I believe Amelia is searching for the Jug of Aquarius. A sacred artifact, one of three Celestial Arcana. There are also the Scales of Libra and the Bow and Arrow of Sagittarius. It is believed that when the Zodiacs fled the mortal plain, the heavens shook so badly from their enemies' assault that the artifacts fell to earth and were lost. I didn't give any credence to the legend but... it would appear that I was wrong."

"So Amelia wants to use the Jug as a weapon against the Zodiacs?" I asked

"It is a divine object created by the gods so it can likely be used against them."

"So how does Ari fit into this equation? Why is Aquarius asking her for help?" Damien asked.

Orion snapped his head up like an idea just occurred to him. "It makes sense actually. The Gifted could never draw on the power of a divine object. Let alone one from the Celestial Arcana. In the hands of a mortal, it would be useless. Only a Zodiac can do that."

"Yes..." Abner said quietly, catching onto Orions thinking . "Or perhaps someone with enough Zodiac power to trick the object so that it could work. Someone who possesses the power of two gods."

Damien looked at me. "Like the Child on the Cusp," he said.

"Precisely."

"But then why attack the Legacies at all if she's been after the Zodiacs this entire time?" asked Argus.

"Because," Damien replied, "she knew we would stand in her way."

Abner sighed. "She's trying to neutralize the only threat to her plan and that's the Gifted and any of their kind."

"Just imagine what Amelia will do now that she knows Ari exists?" Calypso said. "If they are the only two who can draw power from the jug then Ari is a serious threat to her."

"So I guess this means we need to find the jug asap," Damien said. "This is your show now," he turned to me. "What's the call?"

All eyes were on me and I thought my knees might buckle from the weight of the world that had just been dumped on my shoulders. I didn't think I was strong enough to bear it but there was so much hope in their eyes. The last time someone gave me life-changing news in this room, I ran away. I wasn't going to do that this time. Our world was barely surviving because the Zodiacs had disappeared. What would it mean if they ceased to exist all together? I couldn't let that happen. I was Gifted, the Child on the Cusp, a part of something so much bigger and more important than myself. I knew my purpose now and even though it terrified me, I felt like I was finally ready for it. I just had to make the call.

"Let's get to work."

Ashley Kaplan

Aries
Taurus
Gemini
Cancer
Leo
Virgo
Libra
Scorpio
Sagittarius
Capricorn
Aquarius
Pisces

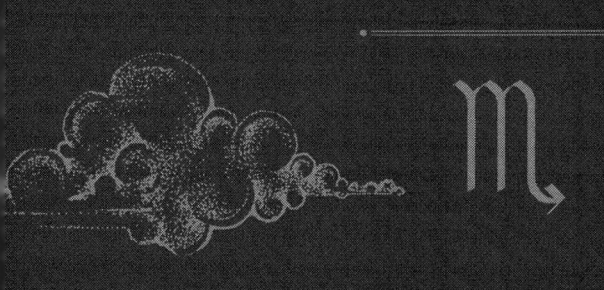

Arcana

"I think we need to go back to the Lee residence," I said. "See if we can find anything to explain Amelia's interest in Jono. I mean, why *this* kid? What's the deal?"

"You'll need back up," Damien added. "I'm coming with."

I gave a nod to him, relieved he would have my back. "Abner, you have a whole thing going with Edgar, might be best if you keep pushing. See if we can get anything else out of him."

"I'll give it my best effort. But we still need to figure out where to start looking for the Jug."

"Well Orion is the resident Sagittarius, can't he track it down?" I asked.

He grinned. "I appreciate the vote of confidence but I can only track something if I come in contact with a place or person it's been with. I can't track something from nothing."

"There has to be some sort of way to extend your reach. What about the book?" I turned to Argus. "Can we somehow use it to get a location?"

Argus looked thoughtful for a moment. "Perhaps. It's possible we can use its magic to broaden Orion's view through astral projection. But there is no guarantee it will work."

"It's a start," I said with more confidence than I felt.

"I'll need some supplies. This will require more than just the book. I will also need someone to stand guard. Once I open the door for Orion, I will have to maintain the connection. If anything goes wrong, I won't be able to pull him out."

"I'll do it," Calypso volunteered. "I can stand guard while you two go in and pull you out if there's a problem."

"Sounds like we got ourselves a plan. We should get going—" I said.

"Arianna, hold on a moment," Abner said. "While I agree that time is of the essence, I think it's wise if we all get a good night's sleep first. The team is tired. You all need a break after what happened today. Physically and mentally. Plus it would do Edgar some good to stew for the night."

I didn't like the idea of waiting until tomorrow to get going. Tracy was missing and I felt like we'd already wasted so much time. But looking around the room, I had to admit that Abner was right. Calypso was still recovering from her fight with the Infernal and everyone else looked exhausted and worn down.

"Maybe you're right," I had to concede. "Rest will do us all some good. I should probably go see Dr. Levine anyway."

Abner shared a look with me that gave the feeling of comfort and encouragement. He believed in me and I had to admit it felt good. As I stalked out of the room, antsy to get going, I had made it only a few feet when I heard somebody call my name.

"Hey, Ari, wait up."

Turning I saw Calypso catching up to me with a warm smile.

"Listen a few of us are going to have drinks at the World's End, you should come."

"I don't know…"

"Look, I know it's been a day. Trust me, I get it. But Abner was right, we could all use a little breather, yourself included. Come with us, it's going to be great."

Calypso smiled at me so hopefully, I couldn't resist and smiled back. She gave a little squeak in delight.

"Perfect, meet us at the pub in twenty."

I had to admit the idea of going out and just having a good time, with no thought to monsters, gods or legacies, gave me a sense of relief. It had been so long since I had seen my friends and done something normal. Yes, this was exactly what the doctor ordered.

Sitting at the edge of my bed, I let out a deep breath, exhaustion seeping through my pores and maybe even fear. Somehow Amelia and her people knew my true nature. Somebody tipped them off but the idea that there was a rat in Astro made my skin crawl. I was beginning to trust these people, learning to fight by their side. Did this mean I had to guard my back with everyone now?

I closed my eyes and fell back on the bed. The backpack on the edge of it shifted with my weight and fell to the ground. With a sigh, I pulled myself back up and slid off the bed to pick up its contents when I noticed my old cellphone lying on the floor. Picking it up, I clicked on the photos folder and scrolled through some better times. Picture of Joel with a foam mustache, and Katie and I dancing in my new apartment. Photos of the three of us at a concert that we snuck out to see. I bit my lip, worrying about what I should do and, against my better judgment, found myself dialing Katie's number. It rang once, twice, three more, and as I was about to hang up, I heard a very breathless voice pick up on the other end.

"Hello? Holy smokes, Ari? is that you?"

I didn't realize the sound of her voice would undo me so much.

"Ari, are you there?"

"Hey Katie, yes." I cleared my throat. "I'm here, sorry."

"Oh my gods, Ari, where have you been? Are you alright? Joel said he saw you with some lunatic—"

"Stop, Katie, stop, I'm ok! Really, I'm fine. Peachy, in fact."

Silence… and then… "What's going on, Arianna? We were worried sick about you. My parents are worried sick about you. They think you ran off to elope or something."

"Elope?" I shrieked.

"The guy in your apartment?"

"Oh the guy, yes… I mean no! The guy is a friend and it's nothing like that."

"Then what is it like?" she asked skeptically. "And who's this friend I never met?"

I sighed again, feeling a new kind of exhaustion, tired of lying to my best friend.

"Katie, please… I don't want to lie to you, but I really can't explain everything right now. I just… I really miss you guys."

"We miss you too," I heard her voice soften from interrogating panic to a calm relief. "We tried calling a few times—"

"I know, I haven't really been using my phone much."

"When are you coming back?"

I closed my eyes to get control of my emotions. The last thing I wanted to do was scare her. So I said the only thing I could.

"Soon. Just wrapping some things up here and I'll be on my way home."

"Wrapping up… this super secret thing you can't talk about?"

"Well, you always said I should find a new hobby," I said lightheartedly.

"I meant, like, painting, not whatever this is."

"Well, what can I say? I'm an overachiever."

"Get yourself home soon, Ari. Wherever you are, just be safe. I love you."

"I will. I love you too."

Hanging up on Katie took a lot of effort and strength. All I wanted to do was spill my guts out about Legacies, gods, and Infernals. About Zodiacs and powers, the Gifted, and Astro City. There was so much I had to let go of; a crushing weight that I needed to unload. But if nothing else, hearing her voice gave me back a little bit of the shaken confidence I felt I had lost.

*

The World's End was a pub in Astro City where all the resident Gifties could be found. There was live music, drinks, and most importantly… games. Nothing like a little healthy rivalry between supernatural humans. I had to smile when I saw the pool table and considered how good I might be with my newfound gifts. *Is that cheating?* I wondered.

"Hey, Ari!" I turned to see Calypso waving me over from a table.

For tonight I had decided to put a little effort into my appearance. It had been ages since I'd gone out for some good old-fashioned fun. It all felt like a lifetime ago now that everything I wore got dirty or blood-stained. But not tonight. Tonight I just wanted to forget that I had this impressive birthright to live up to. I was determined to let my hair loose, letting my wavy brown locks free against my bare back. I'd chosen to wear a green halter top whose earthy tone complimented my tawny, sun-kissed, skin and a pair of dark blue denim jeans that hugged my legs and thighs. I thought I looked pretty good, considering the beating I had gotten a few hours ago.

"Hey guys." I smiled at Calypso. She was having a drink with Orion, Winifred, and Trinity.

Calypso gave me a once over. "Somebody cleaned up nice."

"We can't all look effortlessly beautiful like you," I joked. "Some of us have to put a little elbow grease into it."

"A Giftie who can't take a compliment?" Fred gasped. "Shocking!"

It was nice to laugh with them, joke, and feel at ease. I could feel every part of me begin to relax as we drank and listened to the music. Nobody treated me like I was a freak or a savior for a moment. It had occurred to me then that aside from our team, and now our enemies, nobody in Astro City knew what I was. Looking around the room there were so many people and I was relieved that none of them knew the truth yet. Except for Damien.

Sucking in my breath, I was surprised to see him at the pub. I wasn't sure why though. He needed to let off some steam like the rest of us. I guess I was pretty used to Damien being a loner. Seeing him share a beer with some guys and smiling with ease was strange, out of place. He was wearing a black V-neck t-shirt, a black titanium ring on his right hand, and faded jeans. He looked too damn good.

"I'm going back to the bar," Trinity announced. "Anyone want anything?"

We shook our heads and she bounced off happily, like a bright star in the room that demanded attention.

"Alright," Fred announced, snapping me out of it. "I'm ready to dance." She gave Orion a pointed look but he laughed.

"No way, I'm grounded tonight."

Fred put her hand on his shoulder and looked deeply into Orion's eyes. I could see a spark of celestial blue shine in them as she spoke.

"Come on," she said smoothly. "Have a dance with me, it will be fun."

"Alright, why not?" Orion said slowly.

Fred squealed in delight and began to drag him away. As they disappeared into the crowd, I could just make out Orion yelling over the crowd.

"Hey, using your powers isn't fair!"

I grinned at the two of them. "So it is cheating," I mumbled.

"What?" Calypso asked.

"Nothing, just talking to myself," I grinned. "She's the embodiment of optimism isn't she?"

"Pretty much all of the time," Calypso laughed.

"I have to say, it's pretty amazing, what the two of you have, to be so sure of each other."

Calypso looked at me confused. "Who?"

"You and Orion. I mean you didn't even flinch and he just left with another girl."

"Me and Orion? You mean like, me *and* Orion?" She blinked in surprise and then burst into laughter.

"What?" I grinned. "Are you guys like a secret or something?"

"What makes you think we're an item?" she asked, still smiling.

"I mean, you guys are always together; the way you work as a team is amazing. You're just comfortable, at ease, I kind of admire that."

She shook her head. "Ari what you're describing is nothing more than a very long friendship fostered over years. I love Orion, he's my best friend in the world. But I'm not *in* love with him."

"So…"

"No," she said. "I wish my love life was that easy."

"Ah… I guess there's a heavy past with some guy?"

"There was a guy," she said, taking a shot of tequila. "There was also a girl."

"Also? So wait you're—"

"I'm just me. Not into the label thing. I already have one label to live with, I don't need anymore." She was talking about being Gifted, I realized.

"Besides, when I fall for someone it has nothing to do with their gender. Love is love you know? When it calls, you just have to follow."

"I guess I can't argue with that," I said looking down at my hands. I couldn't look her in the eyes, afraid she might see something I didn't want to admit.

"Why don't you go talk to him?" she asked gently.

"Talk to who?"

Calypso rolled her eyes. "Oh come on, Ari! You and Damien walk around each other like angsty teenagers hopped up on hormones. We're not blind. The guy likes you and, by the way, you were just eyeing him up. I'm gonna say you aren't impartial."

"We?" I asked wide-eyed. "Whose we? God don't tell me, Abner—"

She laughed. "No, don't worry. If it's not Zodiac related, he's pretty much clueless. But… you do like him don't you?"

I shrugged but couldn't help but smile shyly.

"He's not totally unattractive, I guess, if you like that handsome rugged look. Which I'm not saying I do. But if I did… there would be some feelings, yeah."

"So, what's holding you back?"

"It's just so complicated, with this whole birthright thing. He's already had so much taken away from him. And if I… if we… then there would be feelings, and then if I face Amelia and lose… I just couldn't put him through that."

"Well, don't look now, because here he comes. I think I'll go grab another beer."

"Wait, what?" I forced myself not to look but I felt like a deer in headlights. "Caly, stop," I whispered. "Wait, no!" But she was already going. "You're dead to me!" I could see her grin as she disappeared into the crowd.

"Hey Cuspy, did everyone ditch?"

Narrowing my eyes at Damien, I gave him a glare that rivaled his own.

"Keep it up and there will be banners raised with the nickname I give you."

He grinned. "Is that supposed to scare me?"

"Are you scared?"

"I'm downright delighted," he said gloating, obviously pleased that he was getting under my skin. "What do you say to a game of pool?"

I grinned back. I'd been wanting to get at that pool table since I got to the pub. Following Damien, we lined up the balls and he shot first. This brought me back to so many nights the gang and I played back at the university. Katie was the reigning champion but Joel and I could hold our own pretty well. I was pretty sure I could take Damien down a peg and wipe that grin off his face.

"I have to say," I started, lining up my shot, "I'm surprised to see you out tonight."

"What, I can't have a social life?"

"Sure you can, but you're a grouch," I hit the cue ball and landed the red into the left pocket. "So, what's the deal?"

"Maybe I'm just lookin' to have a good time," he said smugly, the corners of his lips rising to a smirk.

"Ah... the age-old tradition of trolling for chicks. Got it. Looking for that elusive good woman, huh?"

Damien lined up his shot next. "I don't believe in a good woman anymore."

"Okay, on behalf of my gender, ouch. That's a little harsh."

"Look no offense but that whole picket fence, apple pie life isn't for me. I've seen enough women in my lifetime disappoint me."

He was looking away from me, still playing the game, but he missed his shot and I was up next. I shook my head sympathetically and moved around the table to line up my shot.

"So, what's your plan? When Amelia is gone and this is all over?"

"This is my life, Ari, it's never going to be over. Even after Amelia, the Infernals are still out there, along with whatever else she unleashed. There will be other threats. Other things to fight."

I paused and looked up at him, realizing how entirely serious he was.

"Don't you want something more though?"

"This is the only life I know," he said simply. "I want to do the job because it's worth doing. We save people, that's a damn good life in my books."

I came around the table beside him and leaned down to take my next shot. Green ball in the corner right pocket. I was about to shoot when I felt Damien lean over beside me, pool stick still in hand, his breath warm against my skin as he spoke.

"What about you? Planning on running off the second this is all over? Back to your friends and your old life?"

I turned my head just slightly. He was inches away from me and I couldn't help but glance at his lips.

"I think... you're trying to distract me... from kicking your ass."

Damien smirked and leaned in even closer. "So what if I am?"

A sudden crash had both of us snapping our heads up as the crowd shifted. There was Jonah, a wide apologetic look on his face and a shy grin at the bartender. By the guy's face, he was more than irritated with the drinks spilled across the floor. Jonah managed to just shy away and zip through the crowd with a weak "sorry!" as he ran off.

"That kid is going to get his if he's not careful," I heard Orion chuckle as he came up behind us, Winifred by his side.

"How does he always manage to get in here?" She shook her head, grinning.

Damien and I looked away and, as it happened, I ended up missing my shot. I couldn't deny that as far as distractions went, he was certainly one of mine. Looking over at Damien, his eyes caught mine and he smiled, clearly amused. I gave him a weak smile back. It was crystal clear that we didn't have a future together. I was unsure if I had one myself anymore, now that Amelia knew I was coming. Suddenly I found being at the Worlds End pub to be pathetically poetic.

The next morning, the teams broke up to get to work. Abner went to further interrogate Edgar. Calypso, Orion, and the Baru were gathering supplies so that Orion could find the Jug of Aquarius through the celestial omina. Meanwhile, Damien and I headed out to the Lee residence to see what exactly was so important about this Jono kid. We were also keenly aware that Tracy was still missing and nobody dared say that it was possible she was already dead. Alex was climbing the walls back in Astro City, itching to get his hands on something to fight. He needed to blow off steam in a big way. I could only hope we would find some clue here that would lead us to Tracy and to Jono Lee.

Getting inside was the easy part, but neither of us knew what we were looking for. Everything seemed neat and tidy with a general oriental decor to the home. There were small oil paintings on the walls of fields and mountains in hues of gold and blue. Beneath them was a shelf with a miniature statue of a white rabbit surrounded by candles. It was almost a scene of worship. I forced myself to look away and move on. To my right, a corner shelf housed several meticulously trimmed potted Jasmine plants and to the left, there was a table covered with them.

"Damien, check this out," I said taking a closer look.

"So what? it's a bunch of plants."

I raised an eyebrow. "Right. A bunch of plants in a home in the middle of a city that rations water."

Damien seemed to be following my train of thought now. "So, how is it that these guys look so healthy?"

"Do you think it's possible the Lees are from the lost bloodlines?"

He shrugged. I didn't know what to think anymore but something was definitely going on here. We continued down the corridor to Jono's room. It was pretty bare – he had a desk, a bed, and a couple of books lying around. There was another jasmine plant in this room as well and a couple of boxes.

"Look's like they were still getting settled," Damien pointed out.

I left him and went on into Mr. and Mrs. Lee's room. There was the same type of emptiness there like they were still moving in and hadn't quite gotten settled yet. The bed was made and the sun shone brightly through the window. There was a closet in the back of the room and I made my way over. Maybe the parents had some sort of secret they kept from their son that would explain things. I reached for the handles and pulled slowly but just as the hinges creaked I heard the unmistakable sound of a sharp gasp and jumped back immediately.

Behind all the hanging clothes, sitting on the floor and hugging her knees was a very frightened and tearful woman. Her long black hair was loose and frazzled like she had been through something. I slowly knelt down on the ground to be at eye level.

"Shh, it's ok. I'm not going to hurt you," I tried to reassure her. "Are you Mrs. Lee?"

She only whimpered but wouldn't meet my gaze.

"Damien..." I called out. "Get in here!" Then in a gentle voice, "Mrs. Lee my name is Ari, this is my friend Damien," I said just as he walked in. "We're here to help."

She only cried harder, shaking her head. I looked at Damien, neither of us knew what to do but it was clear we couldn't leave her there. We had to take her back. Just as I was about to say something, there was a loud crash at the front door and all three of us jumped, startled.

"Hello there!" called out a girl's voice from the other side of the apartment. "We know you're here," she said in a sing-song voice.

I put a finger to my lips as a sign for Mrs. Lee to stay quiet and slowly closed the closet doors. Damien and I exchanged a look before he nodded, ready for a fight.

Axe in hand, Damien took the lead, with me right behind, gripping my daggers. I could just hear the sound of my leather gloves over their hilts as I gripped them tighter. We stepped into the living room. I hadn't been expecting two humans.

"Well," the girl smirked. "I see you came prepared," she gestured at our weapons. Beside her stood a guy, all wrapped in black up to his neck and his face was covered with a mask.

"Who the hell are you?" Damien asked in a threatening tone.

Imani made a face. "Now now, you can put away your toys. We didn't come here to fight. We just want to snuggle. Promise."

"That's her," I said bitterly. "Imani. The one who attacked me at the warehouse."

Imani raised her hands in a gesture of surrender. "We're just here for the woman. Then we'll be out of your hair, no problem."

"You want Mrs. Lee? Why?" I asked.

"That's not really any of your business, is it Giftie?"

"As long as I'm in your way, it is my business."

Imani narrowed her eyes. "Then I'd advise you to move."

"Not really big on taking advice from evil skanks."

"Well then," Imani smirked in a menacing way and cracked her knuckles. "Let's tumble, Cuspy."

The next moment was an explosion of movement as the cloaked guy charged forward, Damien intercepting his moves. I had my eyes set on Imani, expecting her to be fast but I wasn't prepared for the reality. She moved like the wind, quick and silent and my eyes darted around to follow her. In seconds she closed the gap and, with one swift move of her leg, had me flat on the floor, my daggers slamming down under my palms.

I winced and looked up to see her moving down the hall to Mrs. Lee's room. With a stretch of my arm, I summoned a blast of air and knocked Imani forcefully into the wall, and she crumpled to the ground. Behind me, I could hear Damien struggle as furniture went screeching across the floor.

Jumping to my feet, weapons sheathed, I ran to her and grabbed her by the boot, dragging her away from the door.

"Cuspy?" I shouted. "How is this nickname spreading?"

She turned onto her back and kicked me in the knee, making me let go and stumble back.

"I think it suits you," she said as she pulled herself to her feet.

We stood there, sizing each other up, before she lunged at me. This time I was ready. My dagger was in my hand within seconds and I sidestepped her with a slash to her arm.

"That was a warning. Next time I won't be so generous."

Ashley Kaplan

"Fancy moves. Who taught you that? The Professor?"

My eyes narrowed. "What do you know about Abner?"

She smirked. "The question is, what do you?"

Imani intercepted my swipe and knocked my hand out of the way, grabbing my other arm and swinging me over her shoulder. I landed on my back with a wince, breathless. She tried to get past me again to the door but I rolled over and forced myself to stand. With the will of the Zodiac, I slammed the Lees' bedroom door shut in Imani's face and used her momentary surprise to my advantage. I charged at her and tackled her to the ground, the two of us wrestling for dominance. It was clear to me that we were evenly matched but there was no way I was letting her through that door.

We both heard a crash as a lamp broke in the living room. Imani ran to help her partner and I came after her but we both stopped short, staring at the two guys. Damien was on top, axe to the guys' throat. I watched in fascination as Damien tore off the guy's mask and gasped when I saw him staring at the mirror image of himself.

"What the hell?" he asked, shaken. But even as he said it, Damien loosened the grip on the weapon.

That gave his doppelganger enough momentum to shove Damien off him and get to his feet, his fists at the ready.

"Oh my gods, are you Theron?" I asked, taking a step forward.

Imani grabbed my arm with a steel grip. "You already got one of those, this one's mine," she said. With a twist she pulled my arm and knocked me back, closing the space between herself and Theron.

"How are you alive?" Damien demanded.

"Theron isn't available right now, please try again later," Imani said with a smirk.

"What did you do to him, you bitch?" he barked.

"Ouch, words hurt you know." Imani shrugged, "Your brother just upgraded his priorities." Then she turned to Theron. "I think it's time you get going."

He grunted in response but Imani gave him a look that said she was not to be argued with. "Go, I will catch up."

With a last side look at Damien, Theron disappeared through the door and Imani stood to block the exit.

"Get out of my way," Damien warned her.

"Not a chance. meathead."

Damien wasn't going to ask again. He swung his axe at her with such force its speed was incredible. Imani's reflexes were nothing like I'd ever seen and she caught the axe at the hilt, swung around with its momentum, and sent it flying back, the hilt knocking Damien in the kneecap. I watched him crumple and Imani come at him. With a wave of my hand, I raised a wall of current and stopped her short. She banged on it in frustration and glared at me.

There we were again, about to fight, but this time I was ready for her. This time I was faster. Catching her arm, I turned and twisted and in a flash, my dagger was at her side, pointed below her ribs.

"Alright fine, you can keep the mom. She was just a loose end anyway," she said through gritted teeth.

"Why are you doing this?" was all I could manage.

"For justice," Imani replied, this time without a spec of sarcasm or mirth.

"Ari, end it!" Damien growled, demanding retribution.

"Go ahead," Imani chuckled. "Listen to your boyfriend."

"You want me to kill you?"

"If you don't want to look over your shoulder for the rest of your life, I would recommend it.

"ARI!" Damien growled

But I couldn't do it. Imani was human. It wasn't the same as killing an Infernal, a creature that acted on base instinct. She had motive, and reasons, whether they were worthy or not. There was something about her that didn't seem all that black and white to me. The way she talked about justice was genuine; it didn't make any sense.

I loosened my grip on her and she immediately slid out of arms' reach. For a moment, she looked at me with such confusion that I could tell I had surprised her. Her eyes darted to Damien and back to me.

"Big mistake… Ari." With those parting words, Imani disappeared out the door after Theron.

Ashley Kaplan

Aries
Taurus
Gemini
Cancer
Leo
Virgo
Libra
Scorpio
Sagittarius
Capricorn
Aquarius
Pisces

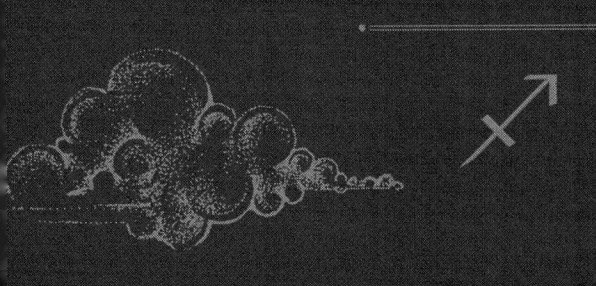

Goodbye

Damien tried to go after her but it was useless. There was no trace of either of them. He stalked back into the apartment and, with an enraged shout, he flipped over a table, his chest heaving.

"Why the hell did you do that?" he snarled.

"Because," I said just as loudly, "we protect people, we don't get to be judge and executioner."

"Well, there's no one else to make those calls. We're the ones that have to make the hard decisions."

"You know what? Killing a person is a hard decision. It's supposed to be. If it was easy, we would be no better than them."

He looked at me with narrowed eyes and a clenched jaw, silent.

"Damien, listen to me," I lowered my voice and stepped up to him. "We will find Theron. But you can't just go killing everyone that stands in your way."

He didn't answer, only averted his eyes.

"Come on. If Mrs. Lee is a loose end, I'd like to find out why. I'm tired of being kept in the dark. It's time to get some answers."

We finally got Mrs. Lee to calm down enough to speak to us. She was still visibly shaken, sitting on the edge of her bed, palms digging into her knees. She was quiet for a long time but finally, she agreed to speak.

"My husband, he can do things. His yéye taught him when he was a boy. Their family was blessed."

"So, he was a Gifted," I said, confirming what I had thought.

"And your son?" Damien asked. "What about Jono?"

She nodded, her face scrunching up as she held back tears. "He has the gift. Such a talented boy."

"Mrs. Lee, we need to know," I said gently, "did you see a young girl here? Her name is Tracy, she was—"

"Yes, yes, the girl was here. She tried to help. They came and took Jono. My husband he tried to stop them. Girl came and hid me, told me to be quiet. Then they were all gone."

"Mrs. Lee, could you tell us… what Zodiac power did your husband and son inherit?"

She nodded and pointed to the small white rabbit statue on her dresser. I looked at Damien in question but he seemed as dumbfounded as I.

"That's a rabbit," I said to her.

"Rabbit is the Zodiac."

"But how?"

Mrs. Lee was actually annoyed enough by that question to look at me. "We are from the Eastern world. Our gods have not abandoned us as yours did. Our people pray to the Eastern Zodiacs."

Damien tapped me on the arm and gestured with his head, asking for a moment. I gave Mrs. Lee a reassuring squeeze and walked away with Damien.

"If what she's saying is true then why did Amelia want this kid so bad? He's not one of us."

I wondered the same thing. It didn't make sense that she would go to all the trouble taking either of the Lee men when they had no part in our war. Mrs. Lee herself confirmed that they did not serve our Zodiacs.

"But if he's not one of us…" I wondered aloud, "then maybe he's one of them."

"What do you mean?"

"Jono can't be the only one who's been gifted by the Eastern gods. Think about it, nobody knows where Amelia got her powers, maybe that's it."

"So maybe she's worried this kid showing up on our playing field could tip us off on where her powers came from," he added.

"We have to tell Abner."

"Alive?" Abner said in astonishment back at the base. "That is wonderful news."

After dropping off Mrs. Lee at the nearest safe house of another Guardian in the city, Damien and I gathered with the team back at the round table.

"But it didn't seem like he recognized Damien or knew him at all," I said.

"It must be a blood spell," Argus shook his head. "Old magics that were kept hidden in the Tetrabiblos. Such spells are dangerous things."

"Amelia did this to him," Damien said accusingly. "I'm going to tear her APART!"

The Baru shrugged but nodded. "It does seem the most likely thing."

"But why?" I asked. "What's the point?"

Abner sighed and rubbed the bridge of his nose, his eyes closed in thought. "I'm afraid I may have the answer to that. I can't believe it didn't occur to me sooner, but of course, it makes perfect sense.

"Abner, you're doing that thing again. Care to share?"

"What? Oh yes, of course. Well, Damien and Theron are the only Gifted Gemini twins that we have with us. Amelia knew that if the two were separated, we would bring Damien to Astro City for his safety."

The Baru's eyes grew wide as he realized what Abner was saying. "Their telepathic bond."

"I'm afraid so. Amelia is using Theron's gift of telepathy with his brother to spy on us. That's likely how she knew we were coming to get Argus, how she was able to ambush you at the warehouse…"

"And how she knew we would be coming for Mrs. Lee," I finished, feeling foolish.

All eyes turned to Damien, now struck with the knowledge that nothing said was safe around him. I could see the self-anger and guilt spread through him with every tense move of his muscles. Of course, he would feel responsible, how could he not? I wanted to reach out and reassure him. Tell him that it wasn't his fault but I knew it was useless. I could tell Damien was shutting down, no longer able to trust himself around us.

"We have to get Theron back. Is there a way to reverse this blood spell?" I asked.

The Baru thought a moment. "I believe I can do it, yes. But I'll need the boy here."

"Okay, then that's a top priority. Orion were you able to see anything on your end?"

Orion looked a little shaken and pale, a result of the extraneous trip he had just taken through astral projection no doubt.

"It wasn't like anything I'd ever experienced, my senses picked up so many different tracks. Like sifting through a bed of straw, each one another lead. This Jug seems to have been all over."

"So where is it now?"

"Cairo."

"As in Egypt? Can we narrow that down a little?"

"I have a vague idea but I will be able to sense it better once I'm there."

"Fill me in later," Damien mumbled. "I have to get outta here." He pushed past us to get out.

We let him go. Nobody wanted to say it but we couldn't speak with him in the room. Not anymore, knowing Amelia was using his brother to spy on us. What was worse is that Damien knew we were all thinking it, so he left. What he needed now wasn't comforting words. He needed action and this information was the best way to help him.

"Abner, is it possible that Amelia has the gift of an Eastern Zodiac?" I said, changing topics.

"I suppose so. Quite possible. In fact, it makes a lot of sense."

"How's that?"

"Well we always knew that other Zodiacs existed in the world but our corner was ruled by our own gods, their magic tied into the very fabric of our existence."

"We know this already," I said impatiently.

"It is because of this unique connection that we cannot receive powers from the Eastern Zodiacs. They are connected to their own part of the world, giving life energy and taking from it in turn. Trying to wield their power could corrupt our souls, such would be the conflict within the mortal that would be affected. So you see it makes sense now that Amelia is Cursed, she is a Westerner. She was never meant to have that kind of power."

"But how can she use the Jug of Aquarius? It's a Western artifact."

"There is quite a bit of lore on the subject. While the gods rule different parts of the world, they are equals to one another. What can be used by one god can, theoretically, be used by another. You'll find there are mentions of these items in other regions of the world as well."

"Like what?"

"Take for example Mesopotamia. They believed that the Jug of Aquarius can summon their god Enki and he would bring forth devastating floods. Then there are the Egyptians that believed a dip of the Jug in the Nile would flood the rivers, signifying the beginning of spring. These are of course Western notions…"

Abner trailed off as he stalked over to the bookshelves once more and sifted through the great number of titles. It was obvious he was quite familiar with the books as he seemed to effortlessly find what he was looking for. After a few minutes of searching, he brought over the right volume.

"Yes, here it is. Specifically, in Chinese astronomy, the lore claims that the water flowing from the Jug is actually not water at all, but the embodiment of an army."

"The army of Yu-Lin," Argus added.

"That's right," said Abner. "A celestial army comprised of forty-five soldiers. They were said to be fierce warriors carrying axes. Called forth from the farthest reaches of the empire and entombed in the jar by the gods."

"So if Amelia can channel the power of an Eastern Zodiac... are you telling me she could summon this army?"

Orion shook his head. "She will be unstoppable."

"Let's recap. The big day is the Observation of the Ascendant," I said. "I think we can assume she's going to use a spell from the Tetrabiblos to open the gates. Then all she has to do is send the army of Yu-Lin to attack," I concluded.

"They won't be like any fighters we've ever faced," Calypso warned. "Our regular foot soldiers won't stand a chance. Only the Astral Warriors will be able to stand against them."

"And we have half their numbers," Orion added.

I could sense the sudden trepidation that gripped the room. We all understood that this could spell the end of everything we knew. Amelia actually had a chance to succeed. But deep down to my core, as sure as I've ever been, I knew one thing with absolute clarity.

"We are going to win."

"That's very optimistic of you Ari," Abner said kindly, "but we can't be sure—"

"It's not optimism. It's a plan. We have a weapon that she won't be expecting."

"What's that?"

"Me."

My entire body felt like it had gone through a meat grinder after my fight with Imani. If she was that strong, I couldn't imagine what it would be like to face Amelia. Back in the war room, I spoke with so much confidence but I was afraid. Afraid to let them all down. I knew that wasn't an option, as surely as I knew that Amelia and I would come face-to-face soon enough.

Amidst my frazzled thoughts, I didn't notice Damien leaning against my door frame as I came up to him. It was a relief to see him; I wanted to be sure he was alright.

"Hey," he said, "can we talk?"

I raised an eyebrow as I opened the door to my room. "Sure, come in."

The way he looked at me as he closed the door behind us had me worried. I thought that maybe I didn't want to know what he had to say.

"Look, about what happened…"

"Damien you don't have to explain," I said quietly.

"As long as I'm here you're not safe, I'm just…" he searched for the words.

"On a mission," I finished for him, understanding. "You need to find your brother. And I—"

"Have to save the world," he said with a half smile that didn't quite reach his dispirited eyes.

"When do you leave?" I asked, but I was only procrastinating, already knowing the answer.

"Pretty much right now. Until I bring my brother back, I can't be in this fight. I have to find him. And you—"

"Have to get to Amelia and find the Jug of Aquarius."

We were just stating the obvious but there was no passion behind the words. My head knew this work was important but my heart… my heart couldn't accept this.

"Damien… you should know. We think Amelia is planning on using the jug to summon an army. If it comes to that…"

I couldn't finish the sentence. Would he be there by our side or could this be the last time I saw him? Looking into his eyes, I saw the unspoken words hanging in the air between us. I saw it in the way he looked at me. In the way he reached for me through the silence. I wasn't ready to say goodbye to him but he needed to go and I had to stay. Damien began this journey with me, being here without him would feel wrong somehow. Although I couldn't get the words out, my body spoke for me. I felt pulled to him with an inescapable magnitude. Before I could think, his hands were on my hips and our lips touched.

When Damien kissed me it felt like the ground shifted beneath my feet. Like we were floating and it had nothing to do with Zodiac Gifts. There was no need for words or promises, there was just this. This perfect moment of his body against mine, his hands, the smell of him. When we finally broke apart, I couldn't open my eyes. I didn't want to see him go and felt him linger for a moment longer. His finger brushed my lips, still warm from his kiss.

Ashley Kaplan

"Maybe in another life…" I heard him say and then all I could feel was the coldness of his absence.

Pisces
Aries
Taurus
Gemini
Cancer
Leo
Virgo
Libra
Scorpio
Sagittarius
Capricorn
Aquarius

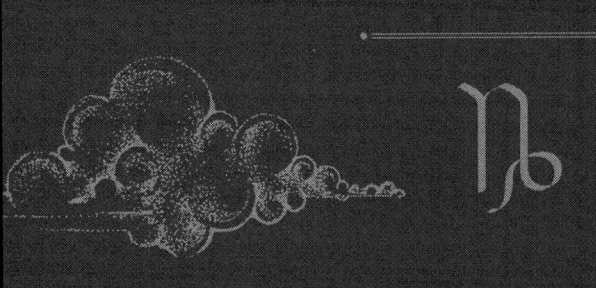

Clash

One of the upsides to living in a fully equipped military city was that we had our very own plane. This was especially useful since we had to fly to Cairo, the last place that Orion had tracked the Jug of Aquarius to. Our team had to take a day to gather supplies, fuel up, and generally gather our strength. Aside from Calypso, Orion, and myself, Abner was coming with us as well as Alex. We had no way of knowing what we'd be walking into but none of us were beset by the delusion that it would be a simple mission.

Abner was our pilot, which was yet another thing I didn't know he could do. The man was an enigma, always sure and collected under the direst of situations. As I watched his steady gaze, I thought I'd never realized how much I relied on his calming energy, how much of that allowed me to push through my insecurities and find my strength. It was a gift that was all his, not given by the gods. It was just Abner.

Once we touched down in Cairo, Orion was able to sense the artifact much more clearly. I had never properly seen him use his gift but it was so different from what I had pictured. He had once described it to me...

"When I conjure the image of a person or item I'm tracking, it's like my body is speaking to the world around me," he said. "I can feel the vibrations in the air that these people or objects leave behind, smells that should be long gone are still there, or tracks that have been weathered by time become crystal clear to me."

Ashley Kaplan

I could see that he was doing this now, his fists closed, only index fingers touching, held up before his face. His eyes shut, brow furrowed, Orion was the definition of concentration. Then he opened his eyes and for a moment they shone with a bright blue spark and then the light extinguished.

"I can see it. I know where we have to go."

Nobody argued. We got in our vehicles, provided by the local Guardians that lived in Cairo, and headed out. We had driven along the bank of the Nile for a way but It wasn't long before Orion had us stopping at a fork in the stream. Stepping out under the hot afternoon sun, he determined this was it, this was the place.

I looked to where the great river Nile had once flowed proudly. One of the longest rivers in the world, it provided food and breathed life into the desert. Now only a stream trickled here. It ran across the deep grooves in the ground that were the only proof of its former glory. Around me, there was no life, only arid sand and the beating sun. We stopped by a formation of boulders, sitting tall just ahead of the split in the river. They were built up to form a sort of cave, its opening black as the darkest night.

"That's it," Orion said. "The Jug is in there. I'm sure of it."

I raised an eyebrow. "In that dark and creepy cave?"

He shrugged apologetically.

"So, who's going in there?" I asked cheerfully.

"I claim the power of seniority," Alex said smoothly. "You're the newbie, you go."

"Yeah, but Calypso is much more stealthy than I am."

She made a face. "But you have that whole birthright thing."

"Children, enough," Professor Abner said in exasperation and rolled his eyes. He unsheathed his sword. "I'll go."

I could have sworn I heard him mumble "babies" as he walked away and inched closer to the entrance of the cave.

Abner didn't have a chance to enter, was only a few feet away when the sand before the entrance blew about and swirled up in a twister, forcing him back. As he rubbed the sand out of his eyes, a woman's voice cut through the silence.

"I wouldn't go in there if I were you. There are nasty things that like to hide in the dark."

There was no shred of doubt, no hesitation in my mind, I knew it was Amelia. She stood there like a queen among her subjects, with an air of unchallenged supremacy. Her hair was loose around bare shoulders and she was draped in a beautiful dress of dark satin. With a smooth wave of her hand, the sand twister fizzled out and dropped to the ground.

Flanking her were the things from my nightmares, two eager-looking Infernals baring their teeth with glee. On her other side stood Imani, ready for battle with her many weapons sheathed and packed away on her person. Not that she needed them in a fight, I thought. Theron was there too, no longer wearing a mask but with a blank expression and beside him…

"Tracy!" Alex roared, seeing his sister at the enemy's side.

He tried to run towards her but Orion and I held him back.

"No Alex, wait!" I urged. "Look at her. Stop, just look."

"She's under the blood spell," Calypso agreed.

Professor Abner came to stand at our side but he was looking at Amelia, speechless. Even as he gripped his sword ever tighter, Abner seemed to watch her in deferential surprise.

Amelia was just as interested as her gaze narrowed only on him. It seemed as though the rest of us were intruding on a private moment that made me feel awkward.

"I suppose I should have known you'd be here Davy," she finally said.

"I imagine you did since you've brought not one, but two of our people. Was that meant to goad us?"

She smiled and I was almost struck by her beauty.

"Why do you always assume I mean you harm?"

I stepped forward to stand at Abner's side. "Your track record sucks, for one reason."

When her eyes landed on me, I felt slightly abashed. Like a child who had just gotten in the middle of her parent's argument. Amelia merely looked at me and it was enough to give me pause. Even I could sense the power she exuded; it made me wary.

"I take it you are the infamous Child on the Cusp, the mighty weapon of the gods?"

As she spoke I could hear the amusement behind each word, like she didn't give the title any credence. Amelia quite clearly did not consider me a threat and facing her now I couldn't blame her. Abner spoke before I had a chance to respond.

"Where is the boy Amelia? Where is Jono?"

"The boy belongs with us, he is not a westerner, therefore no concern of yours. He won't be harmed under my care," she said calmly.

As she spoke Amelia looked me over and that's when we all felt the vibrations spread beneath the ground and all of us took pause. Hot air blew from the cavernous dark behind me and we heard pebbles shake loose as they hit the boulders. Then a horrible sound that wasn't quite a growl, not quite a screech, echoed from inside the cave.

"It may interest you to know that there's a creature guarding the Jug. I likely just saved your professor's life," Amelia said flatly.

"I doubt that," I replied defiantly.

"Watch your mouth," Imani warned.

Amelia only shook her head disapprovingly. "I must apologize but I truly don't have all day. You can either stand aside or be moved."

"You're not getting in there, lady," I said with a confidence I didn't feel.

Annoyance was plain on her face. Without a word, Amelia stepped forward imperiously and it was the cue that her party was waiting for.

The Infernals reared to life, claws outstretched as they charged forward ahead of their master to clear a path. They rushed at us, kicking up sand as they ran and I stumbled backward, shielding my eyes. When I looked back up, I could see Orion with a sword in hand, deflecting blow after blow with magnificent precision. Calypso stood with legs apart, her arms at her side, and conjured two palm-sized balls of fire that she hurled at the Infernals coming her way; they were unstoppable creatures with a thirst for blood.

Ours.

Alex had broken into a run straight towards Tracy, but she only stood there waiting. No warm embrace, not even a look of recognition on her face. Only the cold stare of a warrior ready to battle her brother. This was an impossible fight. Alex could never hurt her, how would he take her down?

Abner caught my eye and gave me a nod to signal that I should go. Amelia was heading towards the cave and Theron walked at her side. For a moment seeing Damien's face on an enemy gave me pause but just as quickly that turned into anger. Anger for Damien and Theron. For Tracy and Alex. My mission was clear; Abner was going to distract her guards and give me a chance to get to Amelia. I saw the professor rush at the younger man and the two clashed into battle. I couldn't worry about that right now, my only target was Amelia.

Racing towards her, I was clumsy in the sand when suddenly a body hurled itself at me and we rolled onto the ground in a flurry. We both regained our footing and stood to face each other. Imani and I going head-to-head once again.

"Stay away from my mother."

"Amelia is your mother?" I looked at her with rounded eyes. "Imani, I don't want to fight you."

"Don't want or afraid to?" she smirked.

Ashley Kaplan

"Afraid? Remind me again, who kicked whose ass last time?"

But this time I wasn't going to hesitate. Willing my strength to return, I pushed my hand forward and kicked up the sand, raising a barrier before me that I couldn't see past.

For a moment there was no movement and then Imani broke through the barrier with a battle cry, jumping down on me with a fist. I felt it connect to my jaw and returned the gesture in kind. Each blow she struck, I was there with a rejoinder or a deflection. I could hold my own in a fight but it was clear that Imani was better than me. I wasn't losing but I wasn't gaining any ground either. We were at a stalemate.

"Tell me Giftie, who are you protecting anyway? Some so-called gods you've never even seen?"

Shaking my head, I looked at her with pity. Imani had been so brainwashed by Amelia she had no moral compass.

"You're wrong. This isn't about them, it's about us. All of us. Amelia's plan can only lead to destruction. I can't let that happen."

"Don't you get it? You're too late."

Wide-eyed, I turned, stomping down the panic that tried to rise up my throat. My eyes darted through the scene until I saw her. Amelia stood at the cave's entrance, blood splatter on her hands. She was cradling the Jug of Aquarius under her arm, the other carefully holding onto the spout and I realized she'd killed the beast that guarded it. No weapons, just her. I watched in horror as she tilted the artifact, its intricate designs illuminating in a brilliant golden light. It shone so brightly that I had to gasp and catch my breath.

A trickle of water began to pour out of the spout until it turned into a steady stream that pooled at Amelia's feet. With delicate precision, the water began to rise slowly and solidify as it formed the vision of a soldier, dressed in traditional Chinese military gear. Then everything went still, and a blinding pain exploded in my rib cage.

I heard the sound of steel against flesh and an unshakable cold spread through my body. My hands reached down to pat my side and, when I looked, I saw that it was now smeared with blood. Imani stepped before me holding a bloodied dagger and I stumbled, falling to my knees.

"I'm sorry Ari. You should have killed me when you had the chance," she said.

Someone was screaming in the background as Imani disappeared. This was the ending I had been afraid of all along. My own weight felt too much to bear and I gave in to it, but instead of hitting the sand, my body was cradled in warm, familiar arms. When I looked up through heavy eyelids, I could see Damien, his body blocking the sun, the rays spread out behind him like a halo.

"Damien," I breathed out, but the effort hurt. "You came... you found us."

"Ari, hey! Hey! Look at me, what do you think you're doing?" he sounded alarmed.

"I think... I might be dying..."

"Nobody's dying, okay? We just have to get you out of here."

"I told you," I spoke slowly, each word a struggle. "This was the ending."

"Listen to me, you can't die. You're the only Zodiac forsaken woman on this earth I tolerate. This isn't your ending, you're too good for this."

With a weak smile, I tried to keep my eyes open. "You don't believe in a good woman anymore, remember?"

Damien's face was blank, like he was surprised to hear me say that.

"Maybe I don't need a good woman, maybe I just need you."

I could barely hear him anymore and, vaguely, I knew that this was what it felt like to die. Every inch of me could feel the life slip through my fingers as the world turned black. As Damien pulled my body up to his, I could see over his shoulder. The last thing I saw was Amelia, Jug in hand, raising her army.

She had won.

*

My eyes opened slowly, expecting a bright sun, but my vision was unharmed. I felt slightly disoriented as I took in my surroundings. It appeared that I was no longer by the Nile but I could hear the strong and forceful beating of water running fast. When I looked around, I spotted a river that was running freely and rapidly. By virtue of its abundance, the ground was covered in luxuriant flora. Grass grew far and wide and there were trees that sprouted from the forest floor.

"Welcome, Ari," a smooth, gentle voice called out.

I had heard her speak before but there had been so much distance between us then. Now her voice was clear and, for the first time, I could see her in the plain light of day.

Aquarius was a vision, truly a goddess that seemed to float on air as she reached out to me. Her hair was done up with fine gold threads looping through the strands; she was adorned in no other jewelry but a simple white dress.

"Come, let us sit and talk. We have but a few moments together."

I couldn't argue with her as we took a seat on a wooden bench by the river.

Ashley Kaplan

"Am I... did I die?"

Aquarius sighed. "It is unfortunate, but I'm afraid so. You see now why we haven't got much time."

"So that's why I can see you now? Because I'm dead?"

"Precisely," she smiled as she would to a child who had gotten the right answer. "This does make speaking much easier. It took quite a bit of effort for me to project my voice in the in-between."

"I failed," I said brokenly. "Amelia is going to win. She's going to come for you."

"Shh, nobody has failed yet, this is merely a setback. But one that has allowed us to speak and I have much to say. I want you to understand why the Cursed One is set on this path of destruction, for it is only by understanding your enemy that you can defeat them."

I listened intently as Aquarius told me the story of a young girl who had fallen deeply in love. With that love, she created a family that lived happily so very many centuries ago. All was well until a nasty plague spread through the land. There were not enough healers, not enough Gifted, to save everyone, and many innocents perished.

"Amelia came to us, begging for our help but you must understand, there was nothing we could do. We could not interfere in the natural order. There are other gods, other deities that rule such things. It is only under unusual circumstances that we might be able to change their fate."

"So her husband... her son... they both died," I said quietly.

Aquarius nodded. "She blamed us for her tragedy, sought out a power that was never meant for her. The gift of the Snake Zodiac corrupted her soul. His magic cursed her. Thus began her reign of vengeance as she hunted down our gifted heroes and freed the Infernals from the darkest parts of the underworld."

"But she was pregnant when this happened. How did Imani survive?"

"How did you?" Aquarius countered. "She is an anomaly, much like you are. There were things we did, we tried to stop her of course..."

"How?"

I stared at Aquarius in a stupor as she explained to me. The revelation that unfolded made me ache for Amelia and understand far more than I ever could. My heart went out to Amelia but I knew this sorrow was no excuse for what she did. As a direct result of her actions, the Zodiacs fled and, with their absence, the world was slowly crumbling.

"So you see," she went on, "you are the last hope. My siblings and I have slumbered for so long that we have forgotten about the world beneath us. It is only through this spirit world that I can be here with you. But we are defenseless in our current state."

"But I don't understand, why did you abandon us? You've got to be far more powerful than Amelia."

"This is true, but Amelia began to corrupt so many of the mortals under our care. My siblings and I were disappointed and hurt by what we took as a betrayal. We had given you land life, safety, gifts of our very own powers. Imagine giving your children all that you could, protecting them, and yet they still turn on you. We could not watch such insolence, such utter disregard for our love any longer."

"But she's coming for you anyway, only now you are vulnerable to her."

"That is why we must send you back."

"Send me back?"

"Restore the celestial artifacts to the realm of the gods. You have the power to do so."

"I don't understand."

"All you have to do is command the item and it will be summoned back to its rightful place. Amelia believes you to be dead—"

"Um, hello? I *am* dead!"

She smiled warmly. "Then you will have the element of surprise."

Aquarius leaned into me and gently blew warm air against my cheeks and face. I realized that she was literally breathing new life into me.

"Good luck, solum," I heard her say as everything went black again.

*

A sharp pain shot through me as my empty lungs filled, begging for air. I gasped, clutching at my chest, my eyes in a wide panic as I felt my body rise onto unsteady feet. Panting, I lifted my shirt and looked down, but the wound was gone as if it had never been. In its stead was a pink scar, a reminder of my near failure.

Anger rose from my core and spread through my bones like an electric current. My eyes searched for Amelia as I took in the scene before me. Calypso and Orion were holding down an Infernal, he was screeching in defiance and flailing his limbs and tail. His brother was splattered in a wasted puddle of ink on the sand. Tracy was laying on the ground unconscious; Alex stood guarding her body from Imani as the two faced off. Just a few feet away from there, I could see Abner sitting on the ground wounded, clutching his leg. Above him, Theron was fighting Damien.

I couldn't believe the relief and sense of encouragement it gave me. My gaze landed on Amelia, still holding onto the Jug, surrounded by a number of soldiers that had risen from their tomb, unbothered by the destruction around her.

Ashley Kaplan

This time I wasn't going to let her rattle me. Despite all that Aquarius had told me I couldn't let my sympathy cloud my judgment. Amelia had to be stopped and I was going to make her feel the true power of the Child on the Cusp. I was ready to come at her with the full force of the Zodiac. My feet carried me over to her and I ignored the gasps and yells as my team, my friends, and enemies witnessed my miraculous rebirth.

"AMELIA!" I shouted.

But Amelia paid me no heed, wouldn't even look up, although I knew she heard. The last shred of my restraint crumbled and let loose something inexplicable from within. With a sprint, I quickly began to close the distance between us, dagger in hand and ready to strike, but Amelia snapped her head up and, with a flourish of her hand, sent a shockwave into my body that hurled me to the ground. My gut felt like it had been punched but I forced myself up. Amelia narrowed her eyes at me and with a calmness to her voice she spoke.

"Stay down."

With another swipe of her hand, a crushing weight slammed by body back into the ground. I felt jagged pebbles dig into me as I dropped and my lip was cut open. My fingertips blotted at the blood now smearing my mouth and my eyes narrowed in determination. I was so sick and tired of being beaten, pushed, and swatted like a fly. Seeing the river bank just feet away from Amelia, there was only one thing I could try now that she might not expect. I reached my arm out, the sun-baked sand scorching my skin, and pointed my fingers towards the stream. Willing everything within me to call on the gift of the cusp sign, I tried to manipulate the water. I could feel the trickle tug towards me, like a magnetic force that couldn't resist my pull. My concentration waned and I felt the pull slip as the water began to rush away from me. Once again I pulled my senses to attention, trying to bend the water to my will. The more I tried, the angrier I was getting. Amelia had beaten me down, Imani had stabbed me and left me for dead. People I cared about were being hurt, kidnapped, and manipulated; I was through playing by their rules. Through with being a puppet to their whims. It was time to make my stand, weakness was not an option; I had already seen what that road led to.

With each defiant thought, my power pulsated inside. Then with all the strength that I could muster, my body hummed as it summoned every remaining drop that ran through the Nile. Such a force beckoned it that the small trickle had now gathered into a great wall, towering over Amelia.

"Aquarius has a message for you," I said through gritted teeth. "She wants her stuff back."

Then I sent the wave crashing into Amelia, watching her disappear inside it. There was immediate relief as my body felt the weight dissipate. I was able to get up and rise. The Jug went flying out of her Amelia's arms and, with a twist of my wrist, I forced the water to cradle the jug and glide it along to where it stopped at my feet.

Amelia was sprawled on all fours and drenched. She looked at me with seething anger, the soldiers she had released still standing like statues beside her. With a low growl, she got to her feet.

"You insolent child, how DARE you?!"

As she rose, the sand around me began to swarm in a circle until it lifted upward into a twister. Just as quickly as it grew, with a smooth wave of my arm the twister disintegrated.

"Neat trick," I said as I turned the twister back around on her and Amelia raised both arms in alarm to shield her face. I let it fall and watched her impotent anger infuse with a knowing fear. I could see the exact moment in her eyes when she realized what she was up against.

"I know what happened to you," I said more gently now. "I understand why you're angry, but you have to know that what you're doing is wrong."

"Just who do you think you are to talk to me like you could fathom... like you know ANYTHING?!"

"You're right. I can't even imagine the kind of pain you must be feeling. But it doesn't have to be like this."

Amelia narrowed her eyes and wordlessly touched her open palm to the ground. The spot shook and then the ground broke open into a deep, dark hole.

"Soldiers of Yu-Lin, I command you to follow," she said low under her breath. The soldiers, living statues, jumped into the hole one by one. Theron followed suit and I quickly looked to Damien where he barely stood, wounded but alive. Imani came to stand beside her mother.

"You may have won a small victory but I have still got my army. You will be seeing them soon." With those parting words, Amelia vanished into the darkness, her daughter coming up behind her.

"Imani!" I shouted. When she turned to me my voice was steady with a promise. "I owe you."

She narrowed her eyes in the same gesture as her mother then she, too, was gone. Swallowed up by the ground as it closed back up around them.

For a moment there was absolute silence. Nobody was sure of what to do or if we had in fact gained a victory here. Damien and Abner hobbled over to me. Orion and Calypso had done away with the remaining Infernal and Alex had bound Tracy, who was still unconscious. They circled me as I picked up the Jug. It seemed like such a plain and insignificant object to have caused all this.

Ashley Kaplan

"Now what?" Damien asked.

"I'm not quite sure," Abner shrugged. "I suppose we take it back to Astro until—"

"No," I interjected. "I'm going to return it to Aquarius."

I turned the jug over in my hands as the things I had heard about it were coming back to me.

"The Egyptians believed a dip of the jar in the Nile would flood the rivers."

"A dip in the wrong hands will summon the vision."

What if it was dipped in the right hands? I thought to myself.

Even as I wondered at the possibility, I was already walking toward the stream. My skin was humming, a reaction to the power that I could feel emanating from the Jug. It was like the artifact knew my purpose and was already responding to my command, the designs on its surface coming to life in an illuminating glow. So bright and beautiful was its power that I was nearly breathless; the air around me felt suspended as I leaned over and dipped its spout into the trickle of water.

We all watched in suspended wonder as the Jug jolted and a cascade of running water was borne. Slowly and surely flooding the Nile until the trickle was a prosperous river.

"My gods," Calypso whispered in awe.

"It's... it's unbelievable," Abner echoed her thoughts.

I stepped away and lifted the Jug up to the heavens as it vibrated in my hands. Perhaps it felt the anticipation of returning back to its owner. The light grew so bright that it blinded us and then the jug was gone, vanished from us, leaving us all breathless as we watched the River Nile flow unchallenged.

Aries
Taurus
Gemini
Cancer
Leo
Virgo
Libra
Scorpio
Sagittarius
Capricorn
Aquarius
Pisces

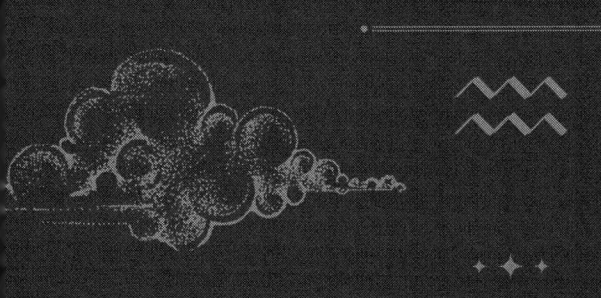

After Death

The next few days back in Astro were a whirlwind of exhilaration as news of our mission spread across the city. No longer a secret, the truth of who I was and what I had done reached the farthest corners of the Western world. Everyone now knew that there was a cusp sign among them and the hope that brought with it could be felt for miles around us. Murphy was especially excited, as children often are, by what he thought was the impossible. I tried to tell him that he lived in a world where the impossible was realized every day, but it didn't matter. To Murphy, I was just "really cool" as he put it, and I didn't want to ruin it for the kid.

After we returned to Astro we had relocated Mrs. Lee to the city as well where she would be safe. I promised myself that I would bring Jono back home to his mother, no matter the stakes. Abner was also curious to speak with her and find out more about the Eastern Zodiacs, he was in full on research mode. Now that we knew where Amelia had got her powers we could possibly find a way to better fight against her. The truth was that the fight with Amelia had taken far too much out of me. I felt like I could barely channel my powers to flick a bug, let alone take on the Cursed One again. A part of me was worried, I felt crushed by the weight of my birthright, but as the days passed I knew my body was recharging. Could feel the ripples of it stretch anew inside my bones and, slowly, I was beginning to regain my strength. The Council of Twelve had higher expectations of me now but I felt like the same girl that had walked into these halls so many months ago. Useless.

Over the following days, we watched closely as reports came in of rivers, lakes, and streams that were flowing again with renewed life. The people outside our world couldn't explain it although the scientists tried. Theories and ideas kept popping up, people trying to explain the unexplainable. Eventually, they would settle on a theory but for now, everyone was in a fervent frenzy over this turn of events. Even the skies opened up as the Jug of Aquarius had blessed us with steady rain once more. It seemed impossible and none of us knew if this was a permanent change but people were excited at the possibilities. We could only hope that the magic of the Jug had changed the course of things indefinitely.

Watching the rain fall, I couldn't help but wish that I could call Joel and Katie. I so wanted to hear the hopefulness in their voices or just sit out in the rain with them with no care for monsters or birthrights. How many stories had we read? How many times had we wondered what it would be like to see a world like this? It was all I could do not to pick up the phone and reach out. Painfully, though, I had to push the thoughts away and forget about them. I couldn't risk their safety by reaching out now. There were too many enemies, too much at stake for that. It was better this way, I kept telling myself, no matter how difficult or how much I missed them.

Although it wasn't quite the same, I still had my friends here at the base to get me through the tough times. Then there was Damien. The first few days after Cairo, he spent trying to track down his brother. And I, in turn, kept my distance. Meanwhile, Orion and Calypso had been trying hard to take my mind off the inevitable. They wanted me to enjoy this win before we faced the reality of the obstacles still ahead.

While I thought that celebrating was premature, I realized that the Astral Army and all the Gifted needed this win. The hope that we could finally turn the tide of this war was too exciting and I didn't want to disillusion anyone. After all, it was hope and faith that helped push people forward even when times seemed their bleakest. Still, there were those of us who couldn't muster the will to celebrate. Alex, the guy I had only ever known to make jokes and smile, sat solemnly those days at the cells where prisoners were kept. That's where they had Tracy restrained, afraid that she would hurt herself. Argus swore that he could undo the blood spell but he needed time to figure out the right ritual and ingredients. It wouldn't be easy but it could be done.

Alex visited his sister daily, without fail, but it was as though she didn't recognize him at all. He came and spoke with her. Some days he only watched while contemplating something. We all prayed to the Zodiacs that Tracy could return to her former self. It was back in those cells where I found him again, sitting with his sister.

"Alex?" I called to him, my voice echoing through the halls.

"Hmm?"

"How is she doing today?"

He shrugged, an intense look of determination and concern in his eyes.

"Abner wants us in the war room. You ready?" I gave his shoulder an encouraging squeeze.

Alex sighed and nodded, giving Tracy one last look before leaving her in the cell.

Alex and I took our seats at the round table where the rest of the team was assembled... except for Damien. I could feel his absence as acutely as that of my strength. The irony was not lost on me. Abner had seemed aged by the whole experience in Cairo, immune to the exuberance around him. He wouldn't be lulled into a false sense of safety. We all knew Amelia was still out there, planning her next move.

"Thank you all for coming," he began in that calm, steady, voice. "While we struck a hard blow against Amelia, it is imperative that we plan our next move while we're ahead."

"Come on, Professor," Orion said with an eye roll. "Can't we just enjoy the moment a little longer?"

"I'm with Orion," Calypso agreed. "We worked our butts off here. Maybe just a few more days of R and R?"

"Abner is right," I said. "We may have won this teeny little battle but Amelia managed to resurrect twenty soldiers. Warriors whose strength is still a mystery to us."

Abner nodded with a grim look. "This is a serious concern. I think we can also assume that she will be after the other two celestial artifacts. Now that we know she can wield the Eastern Zodiacs gift, she will be able to manipulate these artifacts in ways that we can't even fathom yet."

"You mean how she was able to call the Army of Yu-Lin, drawing on the Eastern myths attached to the object where as I was able to draw on the Western myths and flood the Nile?" I asked.

"Indeed."

"Well the Scales of Libra will be perhaps easier to find," Argus said thoughtfully, "but the Bow and Arrow of Sagittarius are far more complicated."

"Why is that?" asked Orion.

"Because there are two parts, the Bow, and the Arrow. There is no guarantee they've not been separated over time. In fact, I wouldn't be surprised if that was the case to keep the weapon from being used."

"And what about my sister?" Alex asked bitterly.

Argus heaved a sigh. "I am still working on it, I assure you. It isn't easy without the rest of the books from the Tetrabiblos."

I knew that we had many hurdles still ahead of us, but hearing it aloud like this made my stomach turn. Looking at their faces, I could see the pain on some, worry on others, and exhaustion that went beyond the physical. I just wanted to take it all away, they needed something to fight for.

"Okay, so priorities – recover the Tetrabiblos and cure the blood spell on Tracy." I turned to Alex with a determined look. "That's number one on my list," I promised. "In the meantime, Orion? I know that astral projection was no walk in the park but we will probably need you to do it again. We have to find those items before Amelia does."

"And then what?" Orion asked. "So we return them to the Zodiacs, but they're still helpless up there, sleeping away this war."

"You're right."

"Uh... Is there a follow up?" he asked.

"As long as the Zodiacs are asleep, they are a target. Abner, you had said we relied on their life force to survive. Maybe what we have to do is wake them."

"Wake the Zodiacs?" Abner echoed.

"Yes! it's the surest way to fight off Amelia or any of her armies; their return to our world. You saw what the Jug did when I returned it to Aquarius. What would happen if the artifacts were restored? Maybe they would be moved to wake, to bring back balance."

"It's possible I suppose. With your ability to use the artifacts we can actually attempt this."

We were only met with silence but there was something stirring in the room. An almost palpable hope at the thought that we could pull off the impossible.

"Look guys, I know it's a lot to take in. Let's take the rest of the day, and tomorrow we'll hit the ground running. Research, recon, retrieval. All the Rs."

With little argument, everyone latched onto the excuse and filtered out, except Abner, who stayed behind to dig through the books and research. It had been a couple of weeks and I hadn't spoken to him much about my talk with Aquarius but I had to tell him that I knew.

"Professor Abner?"

"Hmm?" He looked up from the books. "Oh Ari, you're still here. How can I help you?"

"You never asked me about my visit with Aquarius."

Abner shrugged. "Yes, well, I thought it better to let you tell me when you were ready."

"I think I'm ready. I wondered if I should keep it to myself but she told me things… things that I can't ignore."

His silence spoke volumes; the tension in his shoulders and jaw gave him away. At that moment, I could tell that he knew but he would wait for me to say it.

"I know the truth about you. I know that you're Amelia's husband."

Abner closed his eyes as if to will the truth away and his shoulders sagged. I had never seen him look so much beyond his years. And that was saying a lot considering how many centuries old he was in actuality.

"My family was the most important thing in the world to me," he finally said. "I would have died for them twice over if I thought it would save them. As it happened I did die, but I never dreamed that Asani would…" he couldn't finish.

"Asani, that's your son? Yours and Amelia's?"

"He was an amazing little boy. Always exploring and getting into mischief. The brightness in both our lives. I understand she made bad choices in grief, but Amelia was an amazing woman. This person she is now, that is the curse of the Zodiac. It's not the person I fell in love with. The Zodiacs thought they had no other choice. They bargained with death to bring me back, hoping I could stop Amelia from her path of destruction."

"But it didn't stop her," I said. "It only made her hate them more, that they would use you against her. That they would bring you back but not her son."

Abner hung his head in a defeated gesture. "I miss him every day, more than I could ever put in words."

"And what about Imani? She knows who you are, doesn't she?"

"She knows. I would give anything to have a chance at being her father but she thinks I'm a traitor. That I never truly cared for our family."

"I have to ask... why still fight them? If I had to guess I would say you still loved them. Both of them. Wouldn't it have been easier to turn your back on Astro?"

"There is nothing in this world that I want more than to be at my daughter's side. To hold my wife in my arms once again. But the reality is that the rest of the world will suffer greatly if Amelia succeeds in her quest for vengeance. And I have Murphy to think about now too. I cannot align myself with her, knowing the many lives I would be putting in jeopardy."

Abner was making an enormous sacrifice, just at the chance to save the world. I was overtaken by a deep feeling of respect and immense sadness. There was so much hurt and grief in his past that I didn't know how he kept going. But after this, I understood him all the better. Without a second thought, I reached out and wrapped my arms around him, giving him whatever bit of strength I could. We didn't have to say anything else. I felt him hug me back and, with that simple gesture, I sensed that we both got the courage to make it through to our next encounter with Amelia and Imani.

Emotionally I felt spent, physically even more so. I didn't know how a single person could have so little left in them to give. My bed was calling to me, I just needed some sleep, but when I reached my door, I paused. Just like two weeks ago, Damien was standing on my doorstep, waiting for me.

I couldn't deny that a part of me was excited to see him. The other part was ready with trepidation as I entered my room and walked past him, leaving the door open. Just like last time, I heard it shut behind me, and when I turned to look at him, I realized how alone we were. Here in my bedroom where he had said goodbye to me. Where he had kissed me. The silence just stretched between us as minutes passed by.

"Damien? Why are you here?"

"I'm trying to think of a way to apologize that doesn't sound stupid."

"Apologize for what?"

"I should have come to you sooner, after that whole thing with Amelia."

"You had to go after Theron while there was still a trail to go after, I get that."

"But that's just it." He ran a hand through his hair, frustrated. "There were no leads. I was just desperate and wracked with guilt. He's my brother and I gave up on him. I should have known he was alive, especially with the whole telepathy thing. And then I put you all in danger by staying here."

"How did you find him?" I asked curiously. "In Cairo, how did you know he would be there?"

"Once I found out that he could see me, I realized that I could probably see him too. So I channeled Gemini and tracked him down, but by the time I got there you were…"

"Roadkill?" I offered helpfully.

He winced. "Yeah, something like that."

"So now what? Why are you back?"

"Theron is hiding from me. He must have realized I was able to use our bond against him. It's like he turned it off or something. Argus is teaching me how to block him out too, so they don't get anymore sneak peeks into Astro City."

"That's great…" I said, half-heartedly.

Damien took a few steps closer to me and moved my hair just behind my ear. "I'm sorry, Ari. I know things are complicated right now and I don't want to make them worse. I just want you to know I'm here for you. When I saw you lying there in Cairo, I went a little nuts."

"It's okay, Damien, I never blamed you for leaving. Family is important. But I don't mind you watching my back," I said with a genuine smile.

Damien smiled back. "I have to say you came through, just like I knew you would."

"Except I let Amelia get away and now she will be waiting for me. She'll see me coming and there's so much more at stake now that she's building her army. I'm going to have to come at her with all the force of my Zodiac's gift."

Damien reached out and, with his thumb, traced a line across my cheek.

"I don't think the world is equipped or armored for such a thing."

And then his lips were on mine and I gave in to the flood of emotions. I lost all inhibitions, with no thought to our future, or lack thereof. All I wanted at this moment was to feel alive after the cold emptiness of death. All I wanted was this feeling of warmth and passion as I closed the gap between us and pressed my body to his. Damien's arms reached around my waist and my hands slid into his hair. I was utterly lost in his kiss, could have wandered in it far longer, but he pulled away from me. A gesture I knew quite well by now.

"I hear we have a big day tomorrow," he said gently, "so I'll see you in the morning?"

"Oh... um sure, yeah. See you tomorrow."

After he left, I was a little disoriented, a part of me confused over his abruptness. I thought that maybe... well, I wasn't sure what I was expecting.

With aching muscles, I dragged myself to my window overlooking Astro City. I loved it here at night; the luminescent green of the city lights filled my heart with its beauty. I could feel the magic of the Zodiacs all around me in the air, and I breathed it into my lungs. Somewhere out there, Amelia was looking up at the same constellations as I was but with the knowledge that she had a new enemy. I was keenly aware that the date of the Observation of the Ascendant would come sooner than it seemed, and Amelia was preparing to open the door to the heavens. Since there was no way to stop the astrological event from taking place the only option was to stop Amelia herself.

She would be coming for me now, of that I was sure, but I had something Amelia didn't. I had an amazing team at my side, a fierce protector watching my back, and a wise mentor to help me along the way. After years of searching and waiting, I had finally found a place that I could truly call home and I swore that I would protect it with everything I had in me. I would wake the twelve Zodiacs and restore them to their rightful place. And neither Amelia, nor her hateful creatures, or armies would be enough to stop me.

Aries
Taurus
Gemini
Cancer
Leo
Virgo
Libra
Scorpio
Sagittarius
Capricorn
Aquarius
Pisces

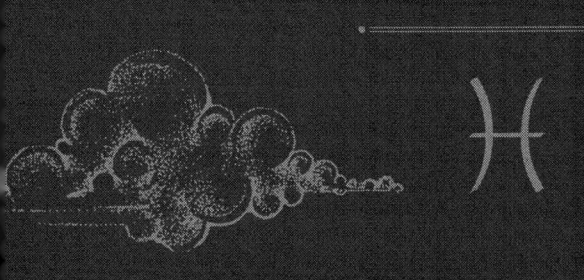

The Zodiac's Gifts

1. **Aries:** Gift of divine weaponry. Can master any weapon and fighting skill. Supernatural reflexes and strength.

2. **Taurus**: Gift of emotional healing, and calm. Can manipulate emotions to sooth their enemies or help those who are grieving.

3. **Gemini**: Gift of air manipulation, can communicate telepathically.

4. **Cancer:** Gift of a shield. cannot be harmed by weapons when they use their power.

5. **Leo**: Gift of fire manipulation and creation of light at will.

6. **Virgo:** Gift of seeing the flaw in any design, can fix anything. Perfectionist.

7. **Libra**: Gift of wisdom and forethought. Can foresee the outcome of any scenario.

8. **Scorpio:** Gift of intuition and clairvoyance, can predict immediate future.

9. **Sagittarius:** Gift of the hunt. Can track anything or anyone.

10. **Capricorn:** Gift of Earth manipulation. Can entice the truth out of anyone.

11. **Aquarius:** Gift of Air manipulation and self healing at an accelerated rate.

12. **Pisces:** Gift of empathy, can feel people's emotions. Water manipulation

13. **Aquarius on the Cusp of Pisces -** / he cusp of Mystery.

Manufactured by Amazon.ca
Bolton, ON